DON'T GO THERE!

Eric M. Palmateer

A Basic Issue Publication

Basic Issue is honored to introduce
Eric M. Palmateer's debut novel,
Don't Go There!

We hope you fall in love with this story and find great joy
sharing and discussing it with your friends and family.

Copyright © 2025 Basic Issue, LLC
ISBN: 979-8-9858922-4-6 (Paperback)
ISBN: 979-8-9858922-5-3 (eBook)
Library of Congress Control Number: 2025903736

Front cover image by Basic Issue, LLC.
Book design by Basic Issue, LLC.
Printed by Basic Issue, LLC, in the United States of America.
First printing edition 2025.

Basic Issue, LLC
30 N Gould St Ste N
Sheridan, WY 82801

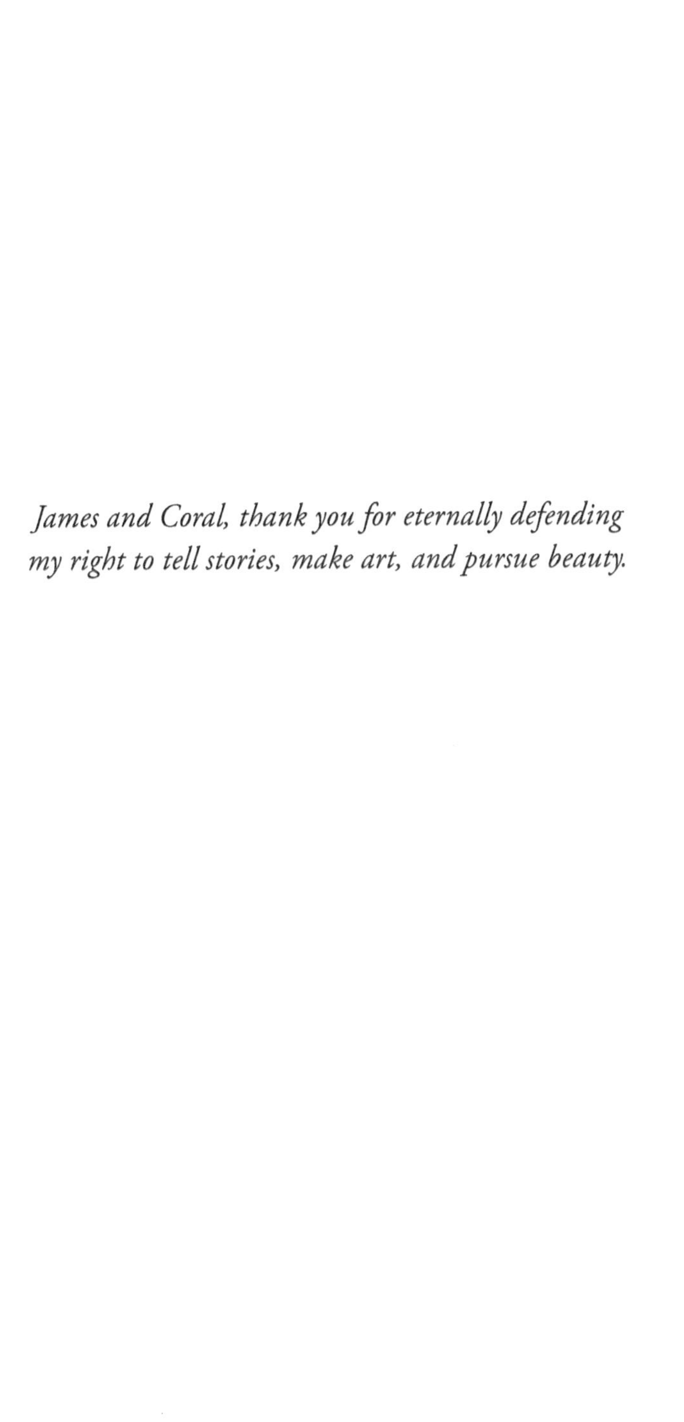

James and Coral, thank you for eternally defending my right to tell stories, make art, and pursue beauty.

1

After Elmo Michaelson had helped North Korea become the most powerful nation in the world, everyone had something to say about his life. However, without a doubt, no one has ever told his story accurately. And, in my opinion, it's always some bullshit concoction of political, cultural, and religious biases that blinds people from seeing the true nature of the man who helped usher in the greatest era of peace the world has ever seen.

Well, I guess Elmo thought I was the only one who could do his story justice. At least that's what he had explained in his letter that accompanied those truckloads of journals, surveillance tapes, and boxes of evidence he had delivered to my house.

Sheesh! I'm glad I'm not Elmo Michaelson. That tall, skinny, American man of Viking lineage. Always chasing some crazy dream or running away from madness. Nope, not for me. I like being here in my cozy office, nestled in the back corner of my house. The scent of coconut candles helping me write. The cool fall breeze from the lake flowing in through the open window. The sound of my son wrestling with his dogs outside. I wouldn't trade my life for Elmo's, even if you paid me a billion Bitcoin.

So, whatever, here goes nothing.

Before becoming the most infamous and misunderstood scientist in the history of the world, Elmo was a simple man with complex problems…

2

ON THE BANKS of the Clinton River, a mile down from a burned-out shipping yard in southeastern Michigan, a 1988 Chevy full-size van sat up on cinder blocks. Old blankets taped to the windows blocked out the afternoon sunlight. On the steel floor in the back of the van was an old mattress in a sea of fast-food wrappers, crushed beer cans, and empty booze bottles. Elmo was alone on the mattress, on one knee, trying but failing to stand up. Both hands clasped his head as he fought to stave off the migraine that threatened to split his skull.

He mumbled a drooling prayer, "Please God. Take my life. End this, please. I don't have the courage to do it myself."

A deep, authoritative drill sergeant's voice rang in his head, "Get up, you son of a bitch! Did we give you permission to quit? Huh? Huh, motherfucker!"

At that point in his life, Elmo had grown accustomed to the voices. The VA had given him pills for this. Deciding to be brave, Elmo resolved to silence the voices permanently. He chewed a handful of Valium and washed them down with a bottle of Jack. He fell backward onto his mattress and sank into the deep, dark vacuum of space—floating free in the loneliest cold imaginable.

Elmo woke with a gasp, covered in curdled vomit, alone on the stained mattress in the back of his van. He felt a hand gripping his shoulder, shaking away the sleep. Then hands grabbed him by the collar of his hoodie, yanked him to his feet, and he smashed his head on the van's roof.

Slightly winded and dazed, Elmo dropped back to his knees, made the sign of the cross over his chest, and cried, "PLEASE GOD! TAKE THIS…"

A gritty, grave voice interrupted, "Zero four hundred. On your feet, soldier! PT time!"

An invisible force booted Elmo in the ass so hard that it launched him into an out-of-body experience. Elmo's thinking, feeling presence watched as something pulled, pushed, and floated his earthly body out the back doors of the van and into the twilight. There, Elmo saw his two years of ungroomed facial hair, a wiry lanky body dressed in a stain covered gray hoodie and sweatpants, and bare feet.

This primal figure started running, fast. He charged up the dirt path, cut through the weeds, hurdled over a sagging knee-high fence, and onto the empty city sidewalks.

His feet slapped the pavement. *Clap phap, clap phap, clap phap.*

Every couple of miles, the voice gave nitro-boost words of encouragement.

"We in this together, motherfucker!"

"I will *NOT* let you quit on me!"

"Ain't a thang! You got this shit!"

"My nigga! Lookin' good!"

A few times, it was phone-a-friend, and the voice called up Grandma.

"Come on, Elmo. I love you. We believe in you."

It all came to Elmo in Dolby surround sound while he watched his body pick up the pace with each infusion of motivation. Drenched in sweat, slime, and vomit, tears flowed from his eyes, and he kept running as the city woke up around him.

On their way to work, the crowds of clean professionals parted like the Red Sea to let this madman freight train keep chugging, unimpeded. The madman extended his gratitude by leaving a wake of rotten apple cider vinegar stench that made people gag after he passed.

Finally, Elmo returned to his van, half-refreshed and slightly winded. He stepped over to his privacy bush, dropped his pants, squatted, and blasted out an intestine clearing diarrhea shit. Fully refreshed. He took off his hoodie and stepped out of his sweatpants and brown underwear. He used his undies to crudely wipe his butt. Then he carried his soiled clothes down to the bank of the ice-cold January river. Elmo fought against the frigid current with each stride and waded out until the water was up to his nipples. He let go of his garments and watched the river carried them away.

A naked man got out of the river, then rummaged through the van to find his old field-sanitation kit. He tore open one wet nap after another and scrubbed every square inch of his pale white body at least three times. Then, he dug out his straight razor shave kit and used the van's side-view mirror to shave off his red beard and the brown hair from his head.

The ropes of shame that pulled his head down disappeared and he stood up to his full six-foot-two height. The twisted knots of anxiety in his chest unraveled, and his shoulders spread broad and strong. He put on the one new outfit he'd bought at JC Penney four years ago. The 34/34 charcoal gray pants were a little baggy, so he walked with his hands strategically in his pockets to hold them up.

Elmo looked up at the sky and asked, "What next?"

And the voice answered, "You're going back to school, fool."

"What am I gonna study?"

With a growl, the voice responded, "Physics… Bitch!"

Elmo looked like Mr. Clean when he went downtown that morning to the city college's guidance counselors and signed up for every class the voice ordered him to complete.

For the next 30,000 hours, the Power barely gave Elmo a chance to resist the mission. It kept him in a near perfect flow state, a passive passenger feeling the painful burn of transformation, unable to affect the direction or acceleration of his life's inertial path.

He activated the same disciplined routines that had served him well when he was training to become an elite intelligence soldier and Korean linguist with the US Army nearly two decades prior. Elmo treated his advanced college math problems as a language with basic concepts that could be mastered following specific, simple study formulas. And language acquisition was something that never seemed to trouble Elmo. He still had a habit of taking notes in Korean because it was much more efficient than English.

Elmo sat in the front row of every class. Closed the library every night. Then stayed up late in the front passenger seat of his van, used the open glove compartment door as a desk, scratched his new growth beard, and pounded his fingers on his graphing calculator. Fatigued, his fingers would shake when they turned off the dome light and paused the physics tutorials on YouTube. Then he plunged into sleep on the clean new mattress located in a sea of textbooks in the back of his tidy van. After six hours of tossing, turning, and fighting nightmare equations, his alarm would go off and he was back at it every day.

In his first semester at community college, Elmo managed a few A-minuses and a B-plus in his math-heavy course load. However, by the time he was accepted by the University of Michigan graduate program, Elmo had a stellar academic record and reputation for being "that guy who hoots and hollers to himself while working out brilliant equations."

Eventually, with his Ph.D. coursework completed and the final draft of his dissertation finished, Elmo sat at the library computer while his cursor quivered, unable to click the 'send' button. Paralyzed by an invisible force, he couldn't bring himself to accept the internship his professors had helped him secure.

Before he clicked it, Elmo closed his eyes, clasped his hands, and prayed, "Our Father…" and the voice gone all those months broke in, "Hey soldier!"

Elmo answered, "Sir?"

"Command been watchin' yah do good. But what chu figurin' prayin' for? Simple. Click submit. Move out, draw fire."

"But sir…"

"Butt sir! You butt sir me? We done checked your heart. And the answer's no. N. O. No. You click that dang submit icon, know what's best for yah. Pull yer head out chir ass. Help some people. Forget it. You ain't got what it takes!"

"Sir, if the Commander only says the word, I can do the mission."

"Lose friends, family, country. You ain't come back from the mission you fixin' fir. You having for that? And besides, I in charge round here! You forgettin' mess I pulled yer narrow ass outta hell?"

"Sir," Elmo replied, "ask the Commander to send me in. I don't care if I come back."

"Cheese and rice, boy! Cheese 'n' rice! So, you gotta have the big one, huh? Well, all fine. Fine. So here be it. Truth be…. Dang! Truth be your real orders cut long ago. Something's in store for you. Some crazy shit you fixed for."

"Sir?"

"Your name, your initials, EMP. Yep, born to be an EMP for peace. But that ain't all of it. Nope. Commander got a special spot for redeemed scoundrels like yah. He knows you doing the physics, the calculations. The machines. Feeling more than good, maybe back, since you done trust no person since that ex-wife done you that way. So yep."

"Sir, I don't understand. My initials aren't EMP."

"Your initials? What! Elmo Michaelson Pow! EMP! Cah pow! Cheese 'n' rice boy. What is about I am saying yah don't understand? Got shit in yer ears. Cheese 'n' rice! You got three life missions! Get you a Ph.D. in physics. Then EMP for peace. Then machines, more specific AI robots that you can love and trust. This gonna be some kinda shit show if I gotta spell everything out fir you."

Elmo scratched his head, nodded in stupefied acceptance, and said, "EMP for peace. AI robots you can love and trust. Okay, I guess."

"What you mean, 'you guess'! Dang, boy! Don't you worry, though. Settle down yourself. I be your battle buddy. Givin' you maps and azimuths. Help you to glory, boy. Ha ha! My nigga!"

"Yes, sir. Thank you, sir. Let's do this!"

That's the back story. Now you know Elmo was called by Providence to get a Ph.D. in physics, build an EMP for peace, and develop AI robots you can love and trust.

It's not his fault most people twisted his story when they tried to tell it. It's much easier to vilify him than to accept the elements of his story that might be a bit hard to believe.

3

Elmo's graduation gown was heavy, starchy, and smelled Febreze fresh. He marched across the creaking squeaks of the portable stage. He followed the cues he'd learned in rehearsal, stopped on the X mark taped on the floor, accepted his diploma in one hand, shook the dean's hand with the other, and held a three second pose.

Cameras flashed.

Elmo Michaelson was officially Dr. Elmo Michaelson, with a Ph.D. in theoretical physics from the University of Michigan. It took seven years of eating-sleeping-living in classrooms, labs, and libraries, but it was all worth it when Elmo defended his dissertation titled:

Biomedical and Social Network Dynamics Associated with Collaborative Research Efforts that Produce Novel Discoveries in the Field of Physics.

Department chair, Dr. Newman, was so protectively possessive of Elmo, his favorite pupil, no one dared state the obvious need to shorten this title.

In truth, no one understood Elmo's Ph.D. research,

but the graduation committee still gave him a pass without challenging any of Elmo's data or methodology. Was it mercy? Sympathy? The department chair's protection? Yes, yes, and yes; however, more than anything, it was Elmo's infectious dreamer's spirit that carried the day.

In fact, the committee got so captivated by the passion Elmo presented his Ph.D. dissertation defense with, they unanimously voted to make him the class's honor graduate.

After the graduation ceremony finished, several committee members, professors, and fellow students approached Elmo and offered to let him join their celebratory lunches. They didn't think it was right that he didn't have anyone there for him on such a special day. However, Elmo declined each offer and said he wanted to be alone with his thoughts.

Elmo stood amid a sea of proud families and friends who snapped photos with their graduates. They shared hugs, high fives, and held hands as they left and made their way to the parking lot.

Once the parade field cleared, Elmo sat on the grass and watched a crew take down the portable stage and chairs. He popped a stick of wintergreen gum into his mouth to maximize the crisp, fresh satisfaction of the moment.

Under his red beard, he had a smile so big it hurt his cheeks. He enjoyed an inside joke that would make him sound crazy if he shared it with anyone else.

4

ONE THING TO remember about Dr. Elmo Michaelson, always expect the unexpected from him. Just three days after graduation, Elmo defected to North Korea to do cutting-edge science free from the crowds of capitalist zombies—addicted to social media, chasing their next fix of salty, greasy food, washing it down with sugary, caffeinated drinks, never sleeping, never dreaming. Nope, Elmo didn't want any of that in his new life as a physicist.

For Elmo, it was an easy decision to take the leap of faith. Years and years of private messages had instilled an unshakeable belief that going to North Korea would align with his greater life mission.

Shortly after he arrived in Pyeongyang, as if guided by manifest destiny, Elmo spearheaded the development of a three-stage intercontinental ballistic missile designed to deliver a truly shocking surprise…

Could he create a missile capable of carrying a miniaturized, boosted, uranium-based, next-generation payload? Of course. But for Elmo's audacious creativity, that wasn't enough. He and his team of North Korean scientists were determined to achieve nothing less than a groundbreaking scientific break-through—one that would transform a highly debated theory into an undeniable reality.

They designed their missile to shoot out of the earth's atmosphere with a flawless flight trajectory and then, upon reentry, look like a failure when they intentionally made the missile wobble and shake. The theory was that the instability would push the fissile material in the payload to reach critical mass. If timed precisely, the resulting nuclear detonation would occur in the Earth's ionosphere and generate a mas-sive electromagnetic pulse (EMP). Amplified by the ionosphere, the EMP would intensify by several orders of magnitude and create an electrical storm capable of frying all modern technology across an entire targeted region—without killing a single person.

That was the theory, at least.

North Korea used the first and only success-ful test of Elmo's EMP missile to make a dramatic entrance into the Global War on Terrorism. The target? Afghanistan.

The strike was universally lauded—99% of Earth's population approved of North Korea's unorthodox contribution. Even the Taliban found themselves oddly grateful as the EMP effectively sent them back to the Stone Age. The only ones outraged were the so-called imperialist 'scum dogs' who ran covert mind-control and terrorist training camps in Afghanistan and northern Pakistan. They lost an entire batch of test subjects to the technological blackout.

But that's a story for another day…

North Korea's Great Leader, Kim Jeong Un, left no room for speculation about his motivations and intentions for the weapon Elmo had gifted his regime. The Great Leader immediately convened an unscheduled Communist Party Assembly and broadcasted his message to the world.

The Great Leader started his address by hailing the strike as the greatest victory for Juche self-reliance since his grandfather triumphantly defeated the capitalist puppet invasion of 1950. Kim Jeong Un added real bite to his rhetoric when he revealed North Korea had fifteen more of these EMP "peace missiles" on standby, deployed throughout the country's vast network of underground facilities, ready to pop out and launch at a moment's notice.

Kim Jeong Un used his newfound leverage to demand immediate, one-on-one negotiations with South Korea—as equals. His vision? Korea would finally determine its own fate, free from the meddling interests of Russia, the United States, or China.

Within a week of the missile launch, the negotiations culminated in a historic agreement: the official end of the Korean War. A twenty-year plan for gradual unification was ratified, built on the pillars of patience, communication, compromise, and peace.

Within a month, all foreign military forces left the Korean Peninsula.

In response to the global enthusiasm for these monumental developments, Pyeongyang was awarded the honor of hosting the next World Cup and Summer Olympics, with North and South Korea competing as a unified team. At Kim Jeong Un's request, the international community agreed to fund the necessary preparations for Pyeongyang to host the events.

To mark the occasion, Kim invited carefully screened journalists from every major international media outlet to cover a three-day world peace extravaganza. The celebration featured a parade of precision-marching soldiers, a perfectly choreographed dance concert, and the inaugural presentation of the Kim Il Sung Hero of the Revolution Peace Prize.

With suspense in the air, cameras flashed and Kim Jeong Un took the stage to announce the prize's first recipient: none other than himself, Kim Jeong Un. The North Korean crowd erupted in a frenzy of cheers to celebrate their Great Leader's unparalleled achievements.

In an unexpected twist, Kim then invited Dr. Elmo Michaelson to join him on stage. He then presented Elmo with the first-ever Kim Il Sung Great Comrade and Friend to North Korea Award. With a flourish, Kim personally pinned the medal to Elmo's chest and, in a display of magnanimity before the largest international audience ever permitted in North Korea, offered to grant Elmo anything his heart desired.

The whole world was there for the taking, but the opportunity didn't overwhelm Elmo. Selfish greed wasn't his driving force. Before becoming a scientist, Elmo had faced rock bottom: bankrupt, broken-hearted, taking buckets of prescription pills, and living in a van down by the river… The divine presence that cleared the gunk from his life still guided him on his sacred mission and gave Elmo his cues.

With the live news cameras rolling and a captivated world anxiously watching, Elmo cleared his throat and asked the Great Leader for a weeklong holiday with Japanese adult film star Sora Aoi.

The Great Leader did not make promises in vain, and he was not about to let such a friend to his regime go unrewarded. Without haste, North Korea made arrangements, and the porn queen flew to Pyeongyang to offer her services to support Elmo's next science project.

North Korea had already announced their national scientific objectives to the world, so it was common knowledge that they planned to have Elmo to build AI robots as his next big project. Naturally, every teenage boy in the world hoped that Elmo intended to invent sex robots modeled after Sora Aoi.

5

Sora Aoi was thirty-two years old and had twelve years in the sex industry. She maintained the nickname "Fountain of Youth" by dedicating hours each day to skincare and staying fit with spin classes, yoga, and Pilates. She regularly topped Google image searches for "East Asian woman," and her iconic look played a role in her fame—she often styled her jet-black hair in a bun held by chopsticks, and her makeup complemented and highlighted her soft, round cheeks, and almond-shaped eyes.

On the night of North Korea's festival, Sora was at the animal shelter, and followed her usual routine: she brushed the dogs, changed the newspapers in their pens, and hung up the closed sign in the front window a little after 6:00 p.m. The shelter was empty, save for her and the dogs, as the other volunteers had taken the night off to follow the latest history-altering news from North Korea.

But something strange broke her rhythm. The dogs, typically content under her care, erupted into a collective, joyous howl she couldn't calm. They weren't rowdy; instead, their synchronized cries seemed almost celebratory, and filled the shelter with an inexplicable energy Sora couldn't ignore.

Sora asked herself, "What the heck has gotten into the dogs tonight" as she settled into the breakroom. She shook it off, and even though she never watched TV, something compelled her to have a little background noise while she enjoyed her tea. Flipping through channels in search of cartoons, she found every station broadcasted an event in North Korea. With a shrug, she muttered, "Whatever," and zoned out with the TV on.

She took a slow, playful sip of her tea and watched the live broadcast of Elmo requesting to have a week-long holiday with Sora Aoi. That part didn't phase her. But when she saw everyone's awkward, boner reactions to the red-bearded American scientist's curve ball request to Kim Jeong Un, she snorted with laughter, sprayed green tea from her nose as she doubled over, and genuinely enjoyed the absurd comedy that this mad scientist just kept on making up.

While she dabbed up the mess from the table with a towel, it hit her, "Oh jeesh, I'm Sora Aoi."

Under her breath, she scolded herself for letting her guard down and allowing this who-does-he-think-he-is Elmo Michaelson's antics to make her laugh without her permission. She made a mental note to dedicate her next Ashtanga yoga session to fortifying the defenses around her heart.

•   •   •

For the next few days, Sora found herself swept up in a whirlwind of surreal, undeniable developments. At her agent's office, she silently prayed as she signed the contract with North Korea, a deal that felt more like a mandate than a negotiation. Sora begged God for reassurance that Dr. Michaelson wasn't a rapey dickhead. She asked angels to protect her in North Korea. She pleaded with the universe to grant her a way out of this life altogether.

Dressed in a baggie gray hoodie and sweatpants, Sora flew into Pyeongyang on a Communist Party private jet. Upon landing, a limo whisked her away to the Ryugyong Hotel, where a black-suited agent carried her bags and escorted her to the presidential suite. Inside, a mobile laboratory and team of lab coat scientists waited.

Like a seasoned professional, Sora followed their directions without complaint. She stripped out of her clothes and stood bare-naked as the scientists busied themselves with their preparations. Their busy hands stuck bio-sensor patches up her spine and on her pulse points, smeared conductive jelly onto her scalp, and attached brain sensors that transformed her hair into a wild, glistening array of spikes and flares.

As per her contractual obligations, Sora completed the preparations by squeezing into the iconic school-girl uniform she had made famous in her debut hit,

Dirty School Girl Shower Spray. Then she slipped on six-inch high heels, which elevated her to an imposing six feet tall.

Sora scoffed at the thought of meeting Elmo being anything more than "Just another sci-fi kinkfest."

6

THE VOICE TOLD Elmo the data from his first meeting with Sora would be the critical foundation for creating his AI robots. He couldn't risk failure, so he wore his best lab coat over his lucky Detroit Tigers shirt. He was also covered in an array of biofeedback sensors identical to those on Sora.

Elmo had arrived hours earlier at the most luxurious ballroom in North Korea. Scientists had meticulously prepared it to meet his precise lab requirements. They had completely cleared out the space, built for a max capacity of 150 persons, except for a single ritzy dining table and two chairs next to three towering, eight-foot-tall computer cabinets at the center of the room. They'd installed sensors and receivers at regularly spaced intervals on every surface of the ballroom, ensuring the onsite computers would collect all their biological signals.

Despite his confidence in the setup, butterflies fluttered in Elmo's stomach as he stood by the computer cabinets and performed one last check on the hardwired connections to the emergency offsite backup system. The checks were truthfully just an excuse to position himself somewhere between the dining table and the grand double doors through which Sora would enter.

Elmo was in a daze and stared at a field of blinking green lights and various sized jacks plugged into his massive computer, when the unmistakable sound of the double doors swinging open caught his attention.

And then, Sora's high heels announced her entrance.

Click.

Click.

The sound echoed, deliberate and slow.

Louder.

Closer.

Elmo scrambled to the dining table to be seated when Sora arrived. So he could stand up to greet her. So he could let her sit down first.

He shifted nervously in his chair, tapped his feet on the floor, and rubbed his thumbs into his palms. Elmo's thoughts raced. He didn't know if Sora spoke Korean as fluently as him, and he only knew a few simple phrases in Japanese.

He tried to assure himself that there'd be little need for talking. It was merely a matter of science. Just physics. Forces. Collisions. Frictions. Projectiles and trajectories.

7

Sora stood outside the ballroom in the Pyeongyang Hotel and gripped the ornate handles of the double doors. She took one deep, deliberate breath, and inhaled so forcefully her ribs felt like they were about to rip apart, then she exhaled as if she was trying to blow out one hundred birthday candles in one breath. Speaking aloud to herself, she muttered, "This Elmo Michaelson is just another white guy with a fetish for Asian girls. Do the work. It's just work. Press the buttons, unlock the magic, and get him off. Then it's over."

With that, she pushed the doors open and stepped inside.

The expansive ballroom swallowed her in its emptiness, and its grandeur amplified her sense of exposure. While she walked toward the center, she felt uncharacteristically vulnerable. The skintight school uniform clung uncomfortably to her body—a costume tailored to be ripped off, not worn as a functional outfit. The jelly-pasted sensors on her skin made her feel slimy and grimy. She felt many things, but sexy was not one of them.

Her high heels punctuated the silence.

Click.

Click.

Slowly.

At first, she couldn't see anyone. The room seemed empty aside from the imposing setup of computer cabinets dominating the center. But the instructions were clear: She was to meet Elmo at a dining table in the center of the room.

As she walked closer, her mind swirled and produced a string of logical things to worry about. She had no idea how to greet Elmo. Did he speak Korean as fluently as she did? Probably not. She doubted he spoke any Japanese, and her own English was limited to a few basic phrases. But she reassured herself: a language barrier wouldn't be an issue because there likely wouldn't be much polite conversation required.

8

Elmo sat as the excruciating nanoseconds passed. Then he quivered. His body vibrated with a strange frequency and amplitude that intensified as Sora's heel clicks got closer.

The clicks stopped.

Elmo's heart stopped.

He saw Sora's head peek around the computer racks.

Elmo stood up so fast he knocked his chair over.

His right hand shot up like he was a second-grader, desperate to answer the question first. "Hi!" he shouted.

With a jerky motion, he lowered his hand.

He stuffed both hands deep into the pockets of his lab coat. A bashful boy.

Elmo realized he was staring at Sora, gawking at all her slim but soft features, his mouth agape. He tried to manually reactivate his natural processes and present a smoother, more gentlemanly demeanor. So, he closed his mouth like he bit into an imaginary muffin and blinked in an unnaturally exaggerated way.

Elmo bent at the waist like a door hinge and bowed a little too deeply. The mechanical pencil in his lab coat breast pocket slipped loose and clattered to the floor.

"Oh crap!" He leaned down to pick it up and…

9

It was only a fifteen-meter walk to the setup in the center of the ballroom, but Sora wondered why she couldn't catch her breath.

Sora stopped at the eight-foot-tall computer cabinets.

She slid out of her high heels. She got a grip on a few solid clean edges of the computer cabinets.

Sora got up on her tiptoes and activated her best ninja stealth mode.

She used her hold on the computers to keep her balance while she inched her head around the corner.

And... *OH NO! Eye-contact! He saw me see him!*

Sora froze, deaf and numb, and watched Elmo stumble, fumble, stand up, flip his chair over, shoot his hand up, blurt out, "Hi," give an awkward bow, and promptly drop his pencil.

Sora unfroze.

She moved with mongoose-like speed and shuffled forward to pick up the fallen pencil.

She bent over, and her outstretched hand met Elmo's hand on the pencil.

Sparks!

Their heads bumped together.

Doink!

Neither picked up the pencil.

Sora sprang upright, wrapped her arms across her chest, hugged herself, and hid her heart. She tilted her head toward the ceiling and closed her eyes so the chandelier wouldn't blind her. *Maybe if I don't move, he can't see me.*

Elmo plop, drop, sat down on the floor and folded his legs like he was in the kindergarten story time circle. He rested his chin on his hands and stared at Sora's feet.

A single giggle popped out of his mouth when he thought, *Those are the longest toes I've ever seen!*

Elmo didn't dare blink, mesmerized by her skin— its creamy hue like a vanilla Haagen-Dazs milkshake blended with bananas. One drop of brown chocolate syrup for a mole on her ankle.

A millimeter at a time, Elmo's gaze traveled up Sora's body. If he stayed on any one spot too long, his heart threatened to pound out of his chest. His body trembled so intensely, a cartoonist depicting the scene would've had to draw him with squiggly lines to capture the vibration.

Sora squeezed her eyes shut so tightly bursts of stars danced behind her eyelids. An invisible gravity rope overpowered her resistive muscles and pulled her head downward, dragging her closed eyes toward Elmo. The strain to keep her eyelids glued shut, like pollen in the wind, floated away, and her eyes fluttered open.

Elmo and Sora's eyes met.

In that instant, their vision zoomed all the way in, crystal-clear and focused. Elmo looked up into the infinite kaleidoscope of Sora's breathtaking, dark brown eyes. Sora looked down at the silk stranded hazel blue cross-stitched patterns in Elmo's eyes.

Elmo smiled, mouth closed, lips stretched ear to ear. Like a happy Curious George with a banana in his pocket.

Sora giggled, soft and bashful. She leaned to the side and corkscrewed one of her feet into the ground. Her puppy dog eyes asked for the cookie she knew she was going to get.

BEEP! BEEP! EARNT! EARNT!

A deafening screech of alarms from the computers shattered the romantic moment, snapped Elmo out of his trance, and yanked him into a critical call to science. He jumped to his feet and dashed to check his scientific instruments.

Sora wobbled on her suddenly unstable legs and plopped to the floor. She crossed her legs, rested her chin on her hands, and watched the action of Elmo going to work.

Elmo's fingers danced and stomped on the computer keyboard. Line after line of code filled the screen until, at last, a progress bar appeared—an indicator that the emergency offsite data processing protocol had been initiated. The computer began transferring every precious byte of biometric data from this fateful date to safety.

Damn the North Korean regime for not allowing Elmo to have the off-site emergency system up and running all the time. Their antiquated communist obsession with conserving electricity threatened to derail Elmo's mission.

The computer calmly exhaled light gray breaths of smoke from its ports. Then it coughed a few ominous clouds of dark brown smoke.

On the screen, the progress bar crept forward. Twenty-three percent... forty-nine percent... sixty-one percent...

Elmo fell to his knees and prayed.

Sora sat cross-legged a few feet away, watched, shook her head in dismay, and hoped the hero wouldn't lose.

A few small sparks flashed from the computer's circuits, and the progress bar clawed and scraped forward.

Eighty-nine percent... ninety-one percent... ninety-three percent...

Elmo pressed his forehead to the floor and pled for divine intervention.

Sora covered her eyes with her hands, but left gaps between her fingers and snuck glances at the unfolding drama.

The computer's robotic voice slurred out a drunken, "Upload complete." One hundred percent.

The computer cabinets all went up in flames. A shrill fire alarm chirped once before the ballroom's sprinkler system activated, dousing and drenching everything.

Elmo sat up from his pose of repentance and water streamed down his face. He looked at Sora seated on the floor a few feet away, equally soaked. Then he looked over at the wet, melty mess of computers. And then back at Sora.

They both made a wow face, like two kids who just witnessed their very first fireworks show.

Elmo and Sora scooted on their butts across the wet carpet, and met under the dinner table, which shielded them from the pitter-patter sprinkler rain.

Sora shivered, her wet school uniform clinging to her skin. Elmo took off his fire-retardant, waterproof lab coat and draped it over them like a blanket.

Wrapped up in the oversized coat, they laid down on the circle of dry carpet under the table. Elmo spooned Sora from behind. Both watched the peaceful rain falling. Their heartbeats, breaths, and every measurable biorhythm aligned in perfect synchronicity.

Elmo tightened his hold on Sora, pulling her close. He pressed a soft kiss to the back of her brain-sensor-jelly-covered, beautiful head. Warmth. Contentment. Security.

Sleepiness overtook Sora and Elmo like a gentle tide. It was nap time after recess.

Sora drifted into dreamland first. Then, lightly snoring and completely relaxed, she let out a short, loud trumpet blast fart.

Elmo was dutch-ovened under the lab coat with Sora. He inadvertently got a nose full of Sora's fart. His last thought before he joined Sora in dreamland was, "Wow! She must love garlic and wasabi almost as much as I do."

10

Adjacent to the ballroom, in a room barely larger than a walk-in closet, six guards crowded around a thirteen-inch black-and-white TV. The grainy screen displayed the live CCTV feed of Elmo and Sora's activities.

Five of the guards had paid hefty bribes to get assigned this duty, hoping for a front-row seat to the anticipated show in the ballroom. Lieutenant Park, the sixth guard, hadn't bribed anyone—he didn't need to. His dad served as the head of the Ministry of State Security, so, you know.

The six men passed a bag of salty grilled squid snacks around, had their eyes glued to the screen, and watched every plot development in the ballroom. The sound of excited, open-mouthed chewing filled the room as the action and drama of the computer fire scene transitioned to the much-anticipated love scene.

The senior guard cranked up the knob on the audio feed two notches below max volume and amplified the sound of the ballroom's sprinklers and every shift from Sora and Elmo.

As Sora and Elmo scooted across the carpet and huddled under the table, the collective chewing slowed to a halt, and no one dared crinkle their hand into the snack bag.

When the couple laid down and disappeared from the camera's line of sight, the senior guard turned the volume all the way up with so much torque the nob broke off.

The six guards leaned in so close to the TV that their heads looked like coconuts lined up in a row. They squinted and strained, dying for a glimpse of a nipple or some pubic hair, anything. All they could see was a rain shower on a five-star dining setup. All they heard was pitter-patter and then…

BRAAAP!

A short, loud, trumpet toot?!

Five guards immediately exclaimed, "Ohhhhh!" like they'd seen the money shot or something. Lieutenant Park didn't rejoice with the others. He shouldn't have gotten mad, but he shouldn't have gotten drunk before reporting for duty, either. This insolent, fast-tracking son of an elite pushed and elbowed his way out of the security room, burst into the ballroom, and stormed over to the couple sleeping under the table.

Lieutenant Park, with his military haircut, rosy cheeks, and steam huffing from his flared nostrils, stood over the sleeping babes. The sprinklers had stopped, but he was still on fire. Park mustered his most severe deep command voice and barked, "Are you gonna fuck this Jap whore or what?"

Sora blinked for a second, then nestled deeper into Elmo's embrace and returned to dreamland.

Elmo, however, woke up completely. He shushed, cooed, and cocooned Sora safely in his lab coat. Once certain Sora was undisturbed, Elmo carefully disentangled himself and moved with the precision of a surgeon.

On his knees, he crouched low, his body tightened like a spring wound to its limit. And like a video game finishing move, he unleashed all his strength and blasted upward with an uppercut that landed his fist in the soft, vulnerable space between Lieutenant Park's jaw and neck. The impact was ferocious, snapped Park's head back and sent him stumbling with a splash into the drenched floor.

Elmo stood tall over his fallen adversary. His chest rose and fell in a steady rhythm. He reached for a napkin from the table to wipe a few drops of blood off his right fist. The young North Korean security officer was limp on the ground. The catastrophic damage to his cervical vertebrae and trachea granted him a swift and painless death.

With not a word, Elmo returned his attention to the dining setup. He slid the plates, glasses, and cutlery to one side of the table, his actions patient and precise. Then he pulled the damp white tablecloth free; its edges trailed water as he lifted it. Without hesitation, he wrapped the tablecloth around Park's lifeless form and folded it tightly and neatly until he encased the officer in a grim, tidy bundle.

Elmo tip-toed back to his sleeping babe and gently woke her with a combination of light kisses on her forehead and soft dreadlock twists of her jelly covered hair. Sora rubbed the dream dust from her eyes. With a warm smile, Elmo took her hand and helped her up from under the table.

They walked side by side and leaned into each other. Elmo's arm draped over Sora's shoulder; Sora's arm wrapped around Elmo's waist. Together they stepped over the human-sized tablecloth croissant and past the smoldering remnants of the computer cabinets.

Elmo held Sora's hand as she played tight-rope walker on the thick braid of cables that connected the onsite data collection platforms to the offsite emergency backup. The couple stopped a few feet from the entrance. They held each other and looked into each other's eyes. Both shared a facial expression that said, "Who are you?" and "I think I really like you."

The double doors burst open and a flood of military uniforms, science lab coats, and Communist Party tan suits flowed past Elmo and Sora. The military uniforms immediately unwrapped the man-sized tablecloth croissant. The science lab coats fiddled with the computer equipment. The tan suits walked around the room with their hands clasped behind their backs.

Elmo and Sora, hand in hand, stepped into the hallway where a pair of agents—a man and a woman—dressed in black suits and grim expressions met them.

Sora's grip on Elmo's hand tightened, and she glanced up at him for reassurance. Elmo didn't flinch. A quiet voice within urged him to stay steadfast and reminded him that his unwavering commitment to the mission would be his salvation.

Elmo gave Sora's hand a gentle squeeze and infused her with the confidence to trust him. They walked in step with the series of clipped commands issued by the male agent, "Walk. Left. Down the stairs. Here. Stop," until they were at the curb in front of the hotel next to a black Mercedes sedan that idled there.

The female agent took the driver's seat, and the male agent opened the rear passenger door for our couple. Before they got in, Elmo asked, "Where we headed?"

The male agent said nothing but answered with a cold, unyielding glare. His silence spoke volumes, but Elmo's eyes lingered on the radio mic clipped above the agent's collar and the coiled earpiece cord that trailed from his neck. Elmo knew the agents were monitored at the highest levels of North Korean authority—perhaps even by the Great Leader himself.

The male agent stood still, held the sedan door open, and was ready to help Elmo and Sora get in the car, if necessary, with force.

Elmo's next words were chosen for him with the

utmost wisdom, and loud and clear, he said, "With the data collected tonight, I have everything I need to complete my next mission. And if you give me time and space to work, I'll deliver an AI capability to the Great Leader, which will be so powerful he can destroy all of Korea's enemies once and for all. Now, please take Sora and I back to my house. Assemble my team of scientists. We must begin work tomorrow morning at zero five hundred."

Dusk set in. Cicadas chirped. No one moved until the agent pressed his index finger to his earpiece and lowered his chin to his chest, listened intently for a beat, then spoke into his mic, "Understood. Yes, sir."

Elmo repeated his question. "Where we headed?"

Deadpan, the agent replied, "You and Sora, back to your house. They're assembling your team of scientists. Work call zero five hundred, tomorrow morning."

The whole ride home, every turn brought them down roads Elmo knew well. It was exactly midnight when Elmo and Sora arrived at Elmo's three-bedroom house located on the outskirts of the Hero of Revolution Kim Il Sung Science Village.

Before Elmo and Sora made their way up the walk to the house, the Communist Party had officially declared the death of Lieutenant Park was an unfortunate accident.

11

Kɪᴍ Jᴇᴏɴɢ Uɴ knew it wouldn't be proper if he allowed an American mutt to get away with the murder of a purebred communist elite's son. Yet, he also intended to milk every drop of brilliance from Elmo's scientific mind before he executed righteous justice. To achieve both goals, the Great Leader crafted the perfect diplomatic approach.

At ten minutes before midnight, Kim Jeong Un hosted Lieutenant Park's dad, Minister Park, along with the brain trust of senior communist officials at the most exclusive venue in North Korea; a dimly lit room in the private basement of Kim Jeong Un's downtown Pyeongyang palace. They'd designed the room to be an exact replica of Al Capone's favorite Chicago speakeasy backroom, complete with a desk, booths, a pool table, and scantily clad women who glided about the room with trays of cigarettes, cigars, and whiskey for the guests.

The communist officials arrived early and waited for the Great Leader, as protocol demanded. Minister

Park and the others sat in silence, their hands absently traced the rims of their full whiskey glasses.

The Great Leader strolled in. He positioned himself at the head of the table and let his gaze linger on each man in turn before raising his glass. "To the Party," he toasted.

The men echoed him and raised their glasses. Kim Jeong Un downed his glass in one shot, while the others took timid sips. As a waitress refilled the Great Leader's glass, he got right down to business and addressed the group,

"We all regret the death of Minister Park's youngest son. Minister Park, if you can accept that your youngest son's death was an accident, then at the next Party Assembly, we will promote your eldest son to a deputy director position and grant him the ceremonial rank of one-star general."

The Great Leader finished and looked at Minister Park for any signs of dissent. Minister Park gave a single, deliberate nod to the Great Leader, then a brief one to each of his peers to signal his agreement.

The Great Leader continued, "Good. We keep Elmo alive until the first time he fails to produce. Then Minister Park will arrange a 'gruesome accident' to kill both Elmo and his Japanese whore.

A murmur of approval rippled through the room.

"This, however," Kim Jeong Un added sharply, "will not distract us from our greater mission. For our Party. For Korea. For the world. No. We move forward.

Right now, the world fears us, and fear breeds respect. Next, they must love us. And hate South Korea. That's the only way our brand of socialism will flourish for our next generation of North Korean comrades."

The Great Leader downed his second glass, refused a refill from a waitress, and continued, "Patience. Get what we need from Dr. Elmo Michaelson. Trust that the Kim family will carry our people to their rightful place in this world. Minister Park, when the time comes, you will have free rein to design justice as you see fit."

The Great Leader looked around at the nodding men. Satisfied with his guidance, he strode out of the room with his hands clasped behind his back, and left his men to have their fill of his top-shelf collection of whiskey and women.

12

ELMO AND SORA stepped into his house and the aromatic blend of rosemary, sage, and basil which grew on every windowsill greeted them. The house wasn't like any other in North Korea. The Party provided Elmo with it as a welcome gift when he was still an unproven theoretical physicist. In their eagerness to woo him, the elites had assigned the design and construction to the regime's top US culture experts, the only comrades who could craft accommodations they believed would cater to Elmo's preferences. Every detail had been meticulously curated based on the intelligence file they'd compiled on him.

The living room and open kitchen floor plan was a replica of the set from *Seinfeld*. One of the bedrooms housed a bow flex and exercise bike. Another room was a home office, complete with an adjustable height desk, a dual-monitor computer, an all-in-one printer, and a cup filled with pens and pencils. Then the master bedroom had one queen-sized Serta mattress smuggled into North Korea past the sanctions, a nightstand with a reading lamp, and walls printed with a blue-sky pattern dotted with glow-in-the-dark stars arranged in constellations. Attached to the master bedroom was the house's only bathroom, which was adorned with marble surfaces and shiny fixtures.

Not to mention the surveillance cameras and microphones in every imaginable nook and cranny of the house. No blind spots. Twenty-four/seven monitoring done from a basement Elmo didn't know was under his house. Shifts of analysts came and went with the network of underground tunnels that led to pretty much every corner of North Korea and many parts of South Korea, too.

Every element of Elmo's life—the meals he ate, the poops he took—all annotated in a written log, tape-recorded, categorized, analyzed, and stored, so a small library was built of his life chronicles in the bunker.

Of all the entries in the activity logs, by far the most thoroughly analyzed was the one from Elmo and Sora's first night together. Here's that activity log as recorded in North Korean history:

00:05—Agents X and Y escort Elmo and Sora from the black sedan, up the pathway, and to the house's front door. Elmo and Sora enter the house. Agent Y assumes watch on the front porch. Agent X takes position in the rear of the house.

00:06—In the living room, Sora rips off her schoolgirl uniform. She wears black lace undergarments. Sora and Elmo enjoy a laugh after she throws her shredded uniform into the corner. The couple embrace, bodies press together, and they kiss as they move across the room. Sora slowly back peddles. Elmo gently presses forward. They halt. Sora undoes a single button of Elmo's Detroit Tigers shirt.

The activity log continued like that until:

00:11—Sora and Elmo shower together and carefully peel the biomedical patches off each other's body, replacing each one with a soft kiss.

A few small details were omitted from the official log. The analyst assigned to transcribe events left his post for an unexcused bathroom break, necessitating his replacement by a more seasoned comrade.

00:21—Sora lies on her back in the middle of the bed. Elmo kneels between her spread legs. He hovers his fingertips millimeters above her skin like he's doing some sort of whole-body static electricity scan with his hands. He appears to brush the tips of Sora's peach fuzz. A look of terror comes to Elmo's face.

00:22—Elmo cups his head in his hands, looks up at the ceiling, closes his eyes, he whispers, "Can I touch you? Can I kiss you? Can I have you? All of you? I can't… I can't touch you… Not unless I hear it… Not unless you give me permission…"

00:23—Sora looks up at Elmo. She has a perplexed smile. A few tears run down her cheeks.

Outside the log, undetectable by cameras, mics, or any other sensor, the words that Elmo spoke, wild and incomprehensible, convinced Sora's heart it was safe to experience true emotions again. Somehow, this plea for consent signaled that Elmo would be careful, patient, and willing to nurture her light to allow it to shine through a series of controlled, wondrous explosions.

00:23—Sora wraps her legs around Elmo's waist. Elmo looks down into Sora's eyes. He hinges his back and gives into the pull of her legs. With both his thumbs, he gently strokes her eyebrows. Sora reaches up and puts her hand over Elmo's heart.

00:24—Elmo looks down. Sora looks up. Both look into each other's eyes. They both close their eyes, then kiss passionately.

The next few entries in that night's log could not give justice to the angles, collisions, forces, and energy fields Elmo and Sora created. Not only because the analysts didn't have sufficient math backgrounds to capture what was happening accurately, but also because they were preoccupied with trying to document the symphony of howls, growls, and panting noises that echoed through the house.

01:55—Elmo and Sora's breathing has slowed significantly. They are wrapped in each other's arms under a fresh set of blankets. It appears they have fallen asleep. (Analyst team lead note: Eight extra copies of tonight's surveillance footage have been made so each individual analyst can perform an independent screening for enemy activity.)

• • •

That night, Elmo found himself in a lucid dream. He stood in the corner of a dark, dank, empty room haunted by soul-crushing cold loneliness. The room was empty except for a door secured by a keypad. Elmo moved to the door like molasses and desperately worked to unlock it. He tried applying the advanced equations from his Ph.D. studies—nothing. He used his unlocked imagination to try EMPs and AI-powered decryption tools—still nothing.

In the dream space, Elmo fell to his hands and knees, and the weight of his despair crushed him. As he surrendered all hope of solving it on his own, the deepest roots of his fierce self-reliance wrenched violently from the core of his being. Tears streamed down his face as a power greater than himself demanded to know why release was justified. Elmo pleaded for just one thing: a simple life with Sora, tending a modest garden and raising puppies. In that instant of clarity, when his heart aligned with his deepest yearning, the door unlocked with a soft click, swung open, and flooded the room with a blinding, radiant light.

Elmo closed his eyes, and in the infinite expanse of his dream, the gravelly voice spoke to him for what would be the last time.

"Congrats due boy! Promotin' yah! But don't be thinking I offerin' call you sir! Haha! But hey, serious, important. So got a big message for you, tell you something a little bit more in-depth for yah today. Hope you gettin' it, too, because here on out, you get commands direct from the tower. Signal go straight to your heart. Not your brain. Certainly not your dick. Message to the heart, then heart calls shots fir dat brain and dick. Now don't let the smart brain fool you otherwise.

"Brain tries to logic some love, all those calculations and, of course, brain be sayin', 'you don't add up, you couldn't possibly do something to fix all your mistakes, and you don't deserve for some goodness.' And of course, if you had to be perfect, a brain logic machine, to get some love, then you never gonna get it. Even if Jesus say He forgive you, your brain say, 'Nope, couldn't be possible, you gotta be chasing the next accomplishment to earn that love.' Don't listen to that brain. The heart, I'm tellin', listen, heart gets the true signal. Then there's your dick.

"Your dick always tryin' convince you love is some dirt bike engine you gotta hump start, and all that exhaustive hip thrusting is worth it when you get that half-second of weightlessness coming off the ramp at full speed. Nah, fuck that shit, too. So, you got it, right? Brain, good and smart. But for love, nope, let yur heart use that brain, not the other way around. And yur dick? Only one place you use it rest of your life, and you won't lose the love allocated by the Savior. Got it?"

"Yes, sir," Elmo whispered. "I think so."

"A'ight. Command already sent your first message. Test out your heart receiver. So, what you get? What come through?"

Without hesitation, Elmo replied, "A simple life with Sora. A small garden. Puppies… But what about my AI mission?"

"Damn! Double damn! Knew hope in you wasn't no waste! Don't you worry about that AI mission. It still coming through you. But heart leads the way. No more my voice. You got that?"

"Yes, sir. And thank you."

"Later, kid. It's been real."

The voice faded, and Elmo stirred. Through squinted eyes, he saw Sora nestled in his arms. He realized he wasn't willfully ignoring any discomfort, nor had his arms lost circulation, even though he and Sora spooned. They fit together better than a pair of Legos.

Elmo drifted slowly but smoothly back to sleep with his internal thermostat regulating his temperature to be perfectly pleasant and allowed him to sleep through the rest of the night without needing to let go of Sora.

13

THE NEXT MORNING, Elmo jolted into the waking world and startled Sora half to death when he sprang out of bed with the urgency of a man late for a revolution. He glanced at the nightstand. The clock radio's big orange numbers read 04:49 a.m.

Elmo bounded two steps out of bed, halted mid-stride, spun on his heel, dashed back to the bed, and planted two quick kisses on Sora's lips. "Sorry, late for work!" he exclaimed.

Sora pulled the blankets up to her chin, wide-eyed, and watched the whirlwind unfold. Elmo, the wild, red-bearded caveman, disappeared into the bathroom, only to reemerge seconds later, transformed into a slick, business beard man. At the closet, he grabbed his clean, pressed clothes. Next, Elmo did a shimmy-dance-button-tuck to become a scientist ready for work.

By 04:54, he sprinted out the front door.

He hurdled off the porch, bolted down the path and hit the streets at full tilt. With about eight hundred meters to the lab at the heart of the scientist village, he ran like a man possessed with the spirit of Prefontaine.

The male agent stationed on the porch, awake and alert but unprepared for the spectacle, sprang into action. Determined to keep Elmo in sight, he gave chase. The agent strained to keep up and huffed and puffed. His elite agent training echoed his orders as motivation.

The two men arrived at the lab in less than two minutes and ten seconds. They both needed a few huffy puff gasps for air and a second to retuck their respective shirts. The agent, for the first time in his ten years of service, felt it was laborious to maintain a stern presence.

Relief washed over the agent when he remembered his duties on the security detail would be complete once he reported Elmo's return to work. He didn't want another morning like it, or any further entanglement with the mad American. Although curiosity about the lab tickled his mind, he decided he'd rather remain in the dark than risk getting swept into Elmo's chaotic orbit.

Elmo caught his breath and gave the agent a sharp salute as a parting gift before he stepped into the lab without a backward glance.

•　•　•

The lab was designed with counterintelligence as a main priority. It appeared to be a two-story building, its exterior clad in tinted glass that simulated windows while they doubled as reflective surfaces, to thwart spy satellites from peering inside. As an extra precautionary measure, a big sign that read "Telephone Company" hung above the entrance doors.

All the lights were on in the big, warehouse-sized room filled with shiny stainless-steel surfaces, glistening test tubes, fancy microscopes, and humming super computers. Eight scientists—four men and four women—had gathered in the conference room, eager to see if they'd recapture the collaborative magic that had led to their groundbreaking work on Elmo's EMP missile.

Despite their unconventional freedom as part of Elmo's team—the most liberated group of scientists in North Korean history—they still adhered to the rigid, standardized appearance expected of their profession: round-framed glasses, unisex mushroom haircuts with side parts, and knee-length white lab coats were their uniform. Each was a brilliant eccentric, their genius often mistaken for traits of Asperger's syndrome, and all had been cast-offs, labeled as useless by the North Korean scientific community, before joining Elmo's team.

Elmo strode into the lab's conference room with a broad, mischievous grin, delighted to reunite with his team. He sat at the touchscreen round table and his eyes gleamed as he looked around at the familiar faces. The men sat on one side, the women on the other, a symmetry Elmo didn't miss. He started from his left and greeted each scientist by their nickname. His voice rang with affection and enthusiasm.

"Old Dr. Jeong, Young Dr. Jung, Rotund Dr. Cheong, Skinny Dr. Chung, Tall Dr. Choe, Short Dr. Choi, Fidgety Dr. Chae, Calm Dr. Chai. I'm so happy to see everyone again. This is the big one. AI. So let's get to it!"

Elmo turned to Old Dr. Jeong, the crafty pirate of the group, and leaned forward with a conspiratorial glint in his eye. "Old Dr. Jeong, can you get us a female Japanese Shiba and a male American mutt? Specifically, they need to be from a pound, and the female must be in heat. We need them by tomorrow morning."

All eyes shifted to Old Dr. Jeong, who traced imaginary dots in the air with his finger and mumbled to himself before he sputtered, "Nah, nah, nah, prah, prah. No problem. Buh, buh, buh. But wha, wha. But why dogs?"

The team exhaled a collective sigh of relief even though they already knew the old scientist could always get anything they needed.

Elmo grinned, "Can you imagine AI robot dogs so flawless a momma dog would mistake them for her own pups? We're going to mate our dogs, and by the time the bitch has her pups, we'll have our AI robot puppies ready to go. Instead of using the Turing Test and relying on humans to certify the authenticity of our AI, we'll let dogs tell us if we got it right."

The whole team broke out in confident nods and a murmured chorus of, "Oh, of course. That makes perfect sense."

From that moment, the lab buzzed with energy. The scientists hummed, whistled, and moved equipment. Each contributed their collective imagination to an ideal AI robot dog production setup.

The next four weeks would be a flurry of accomplishments in the lab. Elmo had his team move forward like a train choo-chooing down the tracks.

And Sora? Well, she was busy too, coming together with Elmo in ways that you'd hardly believe.

14

Sora's initial contract with North Korea had stipulated a week of single-partner productions, with a maximum of three sessions of vaginal intercourse and oral sex per day. There were no restrictions on sexual positions, provided anal penetration was neither suggested nor attempted.

Not surprisingly, immediately after the ballroom "accident," Kim Yeo Jeong, Kim Jeong Un's formidable sister, swiftly renegotiated the terms with Sora's agent. That happened late at night while Sora, oblivious, was fast asleep in Elmo's bed for the first time.

The next morning, as Elmo dashed off to work, Sora lounged on his couch wrapped in a makeshift bedsheet toga. At 5:30 a.m., an unexpected knock at the door jolted her from her relaxation. Kim Yeo Jeong herself stood there to deliver a personal visit. She held a revised contract in hand, with Sora's agent on a cellphone ready to walk her through the updated terms.

Tears of gratitude welled in Sora's eyes when she signed the new agreement. The revised deal transformed her into the star of an ambitious new variety show. Its premise: Sora visiting geriatric hospitals, dressed in traditional Japanese attire from the colonial period, to uplift elderly North Koreans through cultural exchanges. The schedule was grueling—nineteen hospitals in thirty-eight days—but the show's title captured its bold vision: *Nineteen Thirty-eight: Japan in Korea.*

Before 7 a.m., Sora sat dazed in the back seat of a limo, and stared blankly out the window as the summer sun rose over distant mountains. The sweet scent of freshly paved asphalt drifted into the car, and the smooth ride lulled her toward sleep—until *pop pop pip pop bump jump thump.* The limo swerved cautiously down a deeply potholed gravel road and jostled her awake as they neared her first scheduled set.

They arrived at a Soviet-era gray brick hospital that stood desolate in an empty field several kilometers from the nearest city. The structure harkened back to an era when communist planners deliberately left vast empty spaces between buildings for their unrealized, grandiose visions. The driver parked and let Sora out.

When Sora stepped through the hospital's front doors, the stale, mingled scents of old age, kimchi, and thick, musky aftershave greeted her. The source of the aftershave quickly revealed itself: the show's director.

He was a short man, even by North Korean standards, his age marked not just by wrinkles but by the small North Korean flag pinned to his dark suit—a relic presented by the late Kim Il Sung himself. He gave Sora a curt handshake before he marched ahead of her and barked instructions over his shoulder as they walked down a dim hallway with flickering lights and cracked tiles. His hurried tone framed the day's plans as "tactical elements of the production mission."

Abruptly, he stopped, turned to give Sora another brisk handshake, and gestured toward a door with a tinfoil star taped haphazardly on it. "Go in there. Get into role. The Party will tolerate no production delays."

Sora pushed the door open with a creak and revealed an old hospital room hastily converted into a functional, if unpolished, dressing room. Inside, a four-person make-up crew awaited her.

The team, North Korea's most experienced and accomplished, comprised three steady-handed grand-mas and one fabulous grandpa.

The crew guided Sora to a weathered barber chair, adjusted the height with a few pumps, and immediately set to work, their fussy, practiced hands moving with surgical precision.

Sora had prepped for cameras thousands of times before, but it felt entirely different. Before her adult film shoots, she would mentally detach to create distance between herself and the role she was about to play. However, in this present moment, she felt like a little girl cast as Cinderella, swept into a music-filled, magical transformation.

The experience unfolded like a whimsical dance:

Brushes, powders, and glosses.

Spin Sora in the chair.

Snip, clip, and a shampoo dip.

Finish Sora's hair.

The fabulous grandpa, his voice soft with a slight lisp, gestured grandly and said, "Stand up, darling. Time for your kimono. Such a pretty thing, child."

Sora obliged with a playful dance—a shimmy, a twist—to wriggle out of her old gray sweatpants and into the flowing kimono. Like fairy godmothers at work, the crew wisped, swashed, swipped, fispped, and cinched her waist with a perfectly tied bow. In mere moments, the transformation was complete.

Sora turned to the full-length mirror and caught her breath. The image of a chaste imperial princess stared at her. She twirled, and the kimono fluttered gracefully. Sora thanked her fairy god mothers profusely, even as they protested, "Be careful sweetie, you'll ruin your makeup."

She ignored their protests, shook hands, and pulled them in for heartfelt hugs. Her sincerity left them momentarily stunned.

In their over 120 years of combined experience, none of the make-up artists had ever had an actor treat them with such dignity—let alone be showered with the type of earnest gratitude Sora poured on them.

The director called Sora out of the dressing room, put her back on the assembly line, and walked her down the hallway while he re-explained the plan for the day's shoot. "No script. Just a simple meet and greet with an eighty-eight-year-old man, his family, and his doctor. Don't worry. We're sure your presence alone is bound to cheer him up and make for some useful footage."

What the director didn't mention was that the eighty-eight-year-old man was a retired foreign media analyst who had specialized in Japanese culture.

Sora stepped into the hospital room. Cameras, lights, mic booms, and a film crew stuffed into the corners filled the space. At the center was a hospital bed, surrounded by four people—a doctor, two sisters, and a brother—the only ones left on earth who cared enough to spend time with the frail old man lying there, though they privately hoped the old bag of bones in the bed would just do them a favor and die already.

The heart monitor's steady rhythm, *buh beep, buh beep*, told them it wasn't their lucky day yet.

The four people around the bed greeted Sora with the rock-hard smiles which were standard issue for communist TV appearances. Sora returned an over-anxious bow.

The old man in the bed cackled like a goblin. "Welcome! Welcome! The Japanese... Film star... Hahaha! Are you here to make sure this old man's life gets...? A happy ending? Hahaha!"

The old man cackled himself into a tearful fit, and his frail body quaked as if these burst of twisted joy might tear him apart. The sisters, brother, and doctor remained frozen around the bed, their unflinching fake smiles plastered on like masks.

Blushing, Sora curtsied in her big flowing kimono and shuffled up to the bedside. She pulled out her lace cotton handkerchief and gingerly dabbed tears from the old man's hysterically laughing cheeks. Three gentle dabs.

Then the old man jerked his head away from her hand and abruptly stopped laughing. His face shifted into a murderous sneer aimed directly at Sora.

Sora pulled away, rocked back on her heals, and raised her hands like a terrified bank cashier in a stick-up. The handkerchief fluttered from her fingers to the floor.

The old man's sneer cracked, and he erupted into a rattling, wheezing cough. His coughs deepened and his body convulsed, as though he underwent electric shock therapy. His muscles clenched, his back arched so severely it seemed ready to snap. Then, with a gasp that sucked all the air from the room, he collapsed onto the mattress and let out a long, almost peaceful sigh.

"Ahhhhhhh."

The doctor darted to the foot of the bed, stood there, and looked around cluelessly, like he was a failing first-year resident again.

Sora and the family cautiously inched up to the bedside, leaned in, and crowded around the old man's still form. The three siblings' fake smiles dissolved, replaced by tense, hopeful expressions like American football fans watching a Hail Mary that offered a chance to win the game.

The old man broke the tense silence, his breath soft and whispery as his chest rose and fell in a calm rhythm. Slowly, he opened his eyes and blinked as if he awoke from a dream.

He stared up at the ceiling in pure wonder. Then his serenity gave way to urgency. His eyes darted about the room, and with a voice softer yet more desperate than anyone had ever heard from him, he pleaded, "This angel! Where! My angel! Where did she go? Our angel!"

His restless eyes landed on Sora.

The old man's hand trembled as he reached out, and Sora stepped closer to clasp it gently in hers. The old man smiled, nodded assuredly, and repeatedly whispered, "My angel. Thank you. My angel. Thank you."

His family, drawn by the moment, leaned in and placed their hands in to form a pile of warm palms on the old man's chest, over his heart.

The old man turned his attention to his family, and his voice cracked with emotion. "I'm so sorry. Please forgive me. Please, I'm so sorry. For everything. Please."

His eldest sister stared down at him, her weathered face a mix of laughter and tears. In that fragile moment, she saw not the frail man before her, but the mischievous boy who used to help her steal rice from military trucks so long ago.

She replied in a half-laugh, half-sob. "We'll try, you son of a bitch!"

The old man, his family, warm tears flowing, a light sprinkle of smiling laughter. His grip went limp, but the circle of people around the bed kept their tight hold on his hands.

The sound of the heart monitor flat-lined, *beeeeeeeeee.*

Breaking the silence, the old man's brother sang the North Korean national anthem in a slow, somber tone, his voice tender and reverent. One by one, the others joined in. Sora, the doctor, and the sisters formed a gentle chorus. Together, they swayed and hummed, and their voices carried a bittersweet harmony that filled the room.

The director canceled the rest of the day's production schedule. He pulled Sora away from the tangle of hugging and crying around the old man's bed.

Sora, still caught in a dreamlike haze, was ushered into the back of the limo. The director gave curt instructions to take her home and wait for updates on the production schedule.

The limo pulled out of the long driveway and Sora's entire body buzzed like it had woken from a deep pins-and-needles numbness. Every nerve felt electrified. Her eyes, barely able to stay open, were assaulted by colors—reds, blues, and yellows exploded with brain stabbing intensity. The sun-soaked black leather burned her skin like fire, while the arctic blast from the air conditioner threatened frostbite. The sensory overload churned in her head, and she felt like she was about to have a seizure.

She screamed a begging plea to the driver, "Pull over! For the love of God! Please, pull over!"

The driver slammed on the brakes, and the limo skidded to a halt at the end of the driveway. Sora fumbled with the door handle, tumbled out, and landed on all fours in the gravel. Sharp stones bit into her palms and knees as she gasped for air. She felt like Mike Tyson had punched her in the gut, convinced she was dying. Then…

She blasted out a symphony of farts that lasted a spectacular fifteen seconds. Squeakers, horn blasts, pants checking poopers, and a good old silent but deadly. Inside the limo, the driver, windows up and eyes wide, heard every note of the masterpiece—and swore he could smell the master blend she'd cooked up.

Once the wind completely passed, Sora sat, legs crossed next to the car, and looked up at the blue sky and the scattering of friendly, fluffy clouds. She felt completely refreshed and in balance with all her senses, although they were sharper than ever.

She dusted herself off and got back in the limo for the ride home. The driver cast a series of disbelieving glances into the rearview mirror and struggled to believe that such wretched things could come out of such a beautiful woman.

Sora didn't notice the driver's looks because she was too busy playing with the sunroof controls, door locks, and windows. She felt too much like a kid who had permission to be silly with a big, fancy limo ride.

• • •

Back at the hospital, the fabulous grandpa wandered through the empty halls and hummed show tunes to himself while the rest of the crew was busy outside packing up equipment. Guided by an uncanny radar-like instinct he'd possessed since birth, he found himself in the old man's hospital room. He opened the closet door and discovered a young North Korean agent holding a video camera, who had apparently been hiding there all along.

The young cameraman trembled, his cover blown. Ever the opportunist, the fabulous grandpa decided to "soothe" him.

The fabulous grandpa, notorious for his unique transactional arrangements, had never performed a blowjob in North Korea without extracting some form of payment. The young cameraman, toes curled, pants at his ankles, dazed and disoriented, handed over his camera and the priceless footage of Sora's performance without fully comprehending what had happened. His training as a covert operative had prepared him for many scenarios—but evidently not for that. Hiding in closets, it turned out, was a fatal flaw in his strategy.

Once he possessed the footage, the fabulous grandpa retreated to the hospital's empty kitchen, where he watched the recording alone. Something unexplainable compelled him to upload it to the internet immediately. He made use of the encrypted satellite phone with direct connect internet capability that he got from that Army General several years prior. It wasn't hard for the fabulous grandpa to push through the backdoors of the internet undetected.

The video's initial surge in views could be attributed to the title the fabulous grandpa decided on, "Asian angel Sora Aoi gives North Korean grandpa a happy ending." However, within two hours, it had become the most viral video in internet history: over thirty billion views, a billion upvotes, and—shockingly—zero down votes.

The best explanation for the phenomenon came from the top comment, which simply read: "Watch this if you want to see salvation."

By the time the director realized what had happened, the fabulous grandpa's uncensored, unedited upload of Sora's performance had already taken the internet by storm. Damage control was no longer an option.

15

Disney, CNN, Channel One Russia, BBC, you name the media company, they all bombarded Sora's agent with requests for an exclusive interview. A bidding war ensued. However, Sora's contract with North Korea had a clause that prevented her from entering new deals until their variety show launched.

Luckily, Kim Yeo Jeong had been groomed for leadership by her father, Kim Jeong Il, so she knew how to spin any bad situation into an opportunity. Known for her immaculate pants suits, tightly pulled back hair without a strand out of place, and a poker face that could unnerve even James Bond, she was strategic and calculated.

Kim Yeo Jeong sat at her desk and silently laid out her stationery at ninety-degree angles. Sora's agent's name appeared on her caller ID. She pursed her lips and did three methodical blinks before she picked up the call. Kim Yeo Jeong lived up to her reputation when she had Netflix, Sora's agent, and Sora all agree to a $25 million deal that included an exclusive look at Sora and Elmo's new romance, a twenty-episode series featuring Sora promoting wild mushroom tourism in North Korea, and crucially, North Korea's final edit rights before anything aired on Netflix.

Kim Yeo Jeong was probably so effective because she took everything personally. She arrived at Elmo's house with her team and held the teleconference call while she sat next to Sora on the couch. All day, she negotiated until the contracts were drafted, reviewed, revised, and signed by all parties. The deal allowed Sora to restart her life, while North Korea secured 50% of the contract value and all merchandizing rights.

• • •

When Elmo returned home after a long day preparing the lab for the arrival of the dogs and the launch of the AI robot mission, he found his front curb lined with black Mercedes sedans. Although his mind raced with worst-case scenarios, and urged him to brace for trouble, his heart reassured him to stay calm and trust that they wouldn't take away his love.

Sora burst out of the front door, sprinted down the path, and leapt into his arms, which rewarded his faith immediately. He laughed while she planted kisses on every inch of his face.

Elmo gently lowered her to the ground when she slowed her smooches. Sora took Elmo's hand and practically dragged him up to the house. She looked back over her shoulder and giddily exclaimed in her best English, "New deal! Big deal! I love so much!"

And what a deal it was. Kim Yeo Jeong stayed for dinner, and brought her top chefs to prepare both Elmo and Sora's favorite dishes: garlic and wasabi rich sushi rolls, miso soup, and udon noodles. Plate after plate. Stories. A few laughs. A translator helped sometimes while Sora and Elmo found they could connect and communicate by speaking Korean. Sometimes Sora tried English or Elmo tried Japanese, but they returned to Korean to clarify their words, then realized silent eye contact and modified humming were usually the best way to share a feeling or thought.

Kim Yeo Jeong was nearly tempted to let her hair down by the oddly genuine feelings from Elmo and Sora's vibe. Kim Yeo Jeong toasted the couple with a cup of green tea. Busy worker ants cleaned up around the stars unnoticed. The couple accompanied Kim Yeo Jeong out to her sedan and offered profuse expressions of gratitude.

Elmo and Sora had heads and bellies stuffed with the undigested goodness of the day. It was a wash-pajamas-bed-curl up-and-sleep kind of night. They needed rest, for the next day was significant. Their interviews were scheduled at Elmo's lab, where Netflix would get to answer everyone's questions about Sora and Elmo.

Kim Yeo Jeong, however, her day had just begun. She had her driver take her straight downtown to her brother's 1920s speak-easy.

Like so many times before, Kim Yeo Jeong had to take responsibility for an accident she didn't prevent.

•   •   •

Upon entering her brother's room, Kim Yeo Jeong marched forward and took the position of attention a few feet in front of him. On this night, there were no cocktail waitresses or advisors present.

The Great Leader paced pensively in undulating circles around his sister, hands clasped behind his back, and searched for the right words to guide his most loyal subject back on track.

The Great Leader stopped a half meter behind his sister, and he started his address, "My precious Yeo Jeong, what did Father teach us from Machiavelli?"

Kim Yeo Jeong, still and silent, waited for her brother to answer his own question.

The Great Leader continued, "That's right. Father taught us a leader is only secure in his power if his subjects fear and love him above all other things." The Great Leader took a half step forward, put his mouth a centimeter away from his sister's ear, and shouted, "DO PEOPLE FEAR A CLOWN!?!?"

The Great Leader shoved his sister in her back. She did as she should and let the push send her flying into the table and crashing to the floor. She laid there with a pouty weak little girl act that could rival any Oscar-winning performance.

The Great Leader stepped over his sister, so he stood with her lying between his legs. He continued, "Let's play your favorite game. You pray for the Great

Leader to shower you with his blessings, and we'll see just how much generosity he has for you."

Kim Yeo Jeong rolled over to face her brother's crotch. She closed her eyes, interlaced her fingers over her heart, and begged repeatedly, "Oh Great Leader, oh please, shower me with your blessings."

The Great Leader unzipped his pants, pulled out his penis, and sprayed a well-hydrated stream of urine on his sister's face. When he finished emptying his bladder, he gave himself a few extra milks to get every drop to fall on his sister's face. After he gave all his blessings to his sister, he tucked and zipped himself back up.

He stepped over his sister and took a seat at the table. He let his sister lay in her shame for a minute before he barked, "Get up! You filthy whore!"

Moving like an old arthritic lady, Kim Yeo Jeong struggled back into the position of attention.

The Great Leader's scowl melted away, and he rested his head in his hands. He winced in pain. His voice cracked, "Look what you make me do… Sister! What do you have to say for yourself?"

Kim Yeo Jeong collapsed to her knees and bowed with her head pressed to the floor. She groveled, "I'm so sorry, brother! My beloved brother! I'm so sorry!"

The Great Leader winced harder and pinched the bridge of his nose. "Sister," he began, his voice trembled with frustration, "even though you enjoy hurting me. Even though you SCREW EVERYTHING UP!

I'll let you finish your mission. It's only you… It's only you who I can trust.

He leaned forward, his gaze sharp and unyielding. "So, keep Sora and Elmo closer. Isolated. Film everything. When Elmo is no longer useful, we kill them. We have grander plans for the Korean peninsula. For the world. This cannot sidetrack us.

His voice grew cold, resolute. "Our plan only works if we can make all the world's people love us. *And* hate our enemies. The world must beg us to destroy our enemies. Then we'll rewrite history, the real history where we're the righteous victors to be loved, not just feared."

The Great Leader reached for a napkin from the table and threw it at his sister.

Kim Yeo Jeong flinched at the feather-light impact on the top of her head. She stayed deep in her bow and blindly groped for the napkin. Her hand trembled as it closed around the cloth. She clutched it and said, "Thank you for your generosity, Great Leader."

The Great Leader continued his cold address as his sister remained prostrate. "I have at least six weeks of summit meetings ahead. You have no idea how fucking busy I am. While I'm traveling the world, being hosted by the other world leaders, not a peep from you, Elmo, or Sora unless it aligns perfectly with our vision. Our dream. Understood?"

His voice grew sharper, each word sliced through the tense silence. "They must love us and hate South

Korea. We secure the AI, then kill Elmo and Sora. NOW GET OUT OF MY SIGHT!"

Kim Yeo Jeong got to her feet, back to the position of attention, gave her brother a salute that he did not return, then performed a precise about-face and marched out of the room.

Outside, her sedan awaited, with her driver standing at attention. Without a word, she slipped into the back seat, her mind already racing. Back at her office, she stood like a unflinching statue while her servants stripped her out of her soiled clothes and gave her a mechanical wash. Then she threw herself directly into her work. Rest was a luxury she couldn't afford.

Thankfully, she had access to carefully controlled doses of the purest North Korean methamphetamines. They'd keep her sharp and drive her relentlessly toward the next finish line.

16

On their second morning anniversary, at 03:50 a.m., Elmo woke up alone in bed to the clang and clatter of Sora in the kitchen. He stretched, scratched his head, and yawned his way into the kitchen. There she was, intently focused on pouring brown foam to the brim of a mug.

She looked up, caught sight of him, and smiled warmly. "Come, come, coffee!" she said.

Elmo settled on a stool at the kitchen bar, and Sora joined him. They sipped in silence, their eyes closed with each soothing taste. That was their last moment of calm for the day.

Getting ready together was a clumsy dance. They bumped into each other in the hallway, misjudged turns, and shared brief laughter over misplaced items. Somehow, they managed to leave early, and had a peaceful walk, hand in hand, to the lab.

Their pace was slow, their minds distant, lost in a swirl of thoughts. From time to time, they glanced at each other, caught in a quick cycle of worry: *Should I say something? Should I break the silence? No… It's fine. I just like being near this person.* Followed by an awkward but anxiety-relieving, nervous laugh.

When they arrived at the lab, the calm dissolved entirely. Visitors swarmed the building. Production vans and trucks lined the front entrance, and their hulking presence nearly blocked the doorway. Inside, equipment, sprawled chaotically, wove around the lab like an invasive vine, threatening to choke the science inside.

Kim Yeo Jeong had assigned herself the role of director, producer, and chief editor for the project. She waited for Elmo and Sora, ready to address any of their consternations.

For Elmo, it was the AI project; he did not approve of all the uncalculated variables in his lab. But when he looked at the stars in Sora's eyes, his heart told him to let go and go with the flow.

Sora, meanwhile, worried about Kim Yeo Jeong taking on too much responsibility in the production and not having the right qualifications for this important project.

Kim Yeo Jeong immediately detected her star's trepidations and knew how to best assuage Sora's worries. After they exchanged greetings, Kim Yeo Jeong turned to Elmo. "Tell Sora what you know about me from your time in military intelligence."

Elmo smiled and replied, "Sora, you don't have to worry. Kim Yeo Jeong always does her homework. At least she did when she was the top pupil in her film, fashion, and art classes all those years she lived in Paris under the name Kim Jiyon."

Sora looked at Elmo with her mouth agape and an expression that said, *I didn't know you could do that*, but there was no time for explanations as Kim Yeo Jeong rushed the couple over to makeup. "Elmo, you need little makeup or time on the camera. Your priority is AI. So you're up first."

Brushes and powders. Soften the edges, even out the skin tone. And Elmo was ready.

The scientists had already cleared out a corner of the lab the day before, but that was to make room for the dogs. The production crew, unaware of that, had commandeered the space for their purposes and transformed it into an interview set, complete with a couch between two large ferns.

While a staff member clipped a microphone to his shirt, Elmo glanced over their shoulder. At the entrance, he spotted Old Dr. Jeong, accompanied by four unfamiliar men in military uniforms, carrying dog kennels.

Elmo took his place on the interview couch, his curiosity piqued. Through the glare of the lights and the lenses of the cameras, he watched the soldiers accept small pouches from Old Dr. Jeong before they left the scientist behind with the kennels.

Old Dr. Jeong noticed Elmo and gave him a cheerful wave. Elmo grinned, returned the gesture, and added a big, exaggerated shrug that said, *I don't know where to put the dogs. You can figure it out.*

The doctor sighed, and his shoulders slumped before he raised a finger and traced imaginary lines in the air, clearly brainstorming a solution to the new problem.

Meanwhile, the interviewer took her seat beside Elmo. She was a figure of quiet authority, often called the North Korean Barbara Walters—a kindly older woman whose disarming demeanor made her a master at delivering hard-hitting questions.

The lights got brighter. Kim Yeo Jeong took a seat in the director's seat. "And… action!"

Elmo looked like a deer in the headlights when the interviewer began in a warm, rosy tone. "Dr. Elmo Michaelson, what a pleasure to have you with us today. Where should we begin? Ph.D.—wow. The peace missile that saved North Korea from the constant threat of invasion—double wow. Former US intelligence… and now, true love? You're a man we simply must get to know."

Elmo nodded along, and listened intently to her words, but his eyes darted toward Old Dr. Jeong. The elderly scientist still awkwardly shuffled around the room, unsure where to place the dog kennels.

Despite the distraction, Elmo didn't leave the interviewer hanging. He shook his head vigorously and jumped in. "Yeah, yeah. All that. Yeah. But now it's AI robot dogs you can love and trust…"

The words hung in the air. Elmo froze, realizing he'd just revealed a key detail about his project—one he hadn't disclosed to anyone outside his team. He knew, of course, that the regime already knew. Nothing escaped their surveillance. But to reveal the information to the public? That was a different matter entirely.

In her director's chair, Kim Yeo Jeong sat up straighter, her expression unreadable. *Does the entire interview need to be reshot?* she wondered. The interviewer, meanwhile, shot Elmo a sharp look, her irritation barely masked.

But Kim Yeo Jeong wasn't about to stop the momentum. She extended a commanding finger toward the crew and signaled, "Keep shooting. Keep filming."

The interviewer straightened her pants suit and pressed on with her line of questions. Elmo remained on the couch, squinted past the cameras and lights, and his attention drifted toward the commotion around Old Dr. Jeong and the dog kennels.

Her next few questions barely registered with Elmo. Annoyance flashed across her face, and finally, the North Korean Barbara Walters snapped her fingers sharply in front of his eyes. "Dr. Michaelson! Dr. Michaelson!"

Elmo shook the dizziness from his head, looked at the North Korean Barbara Walters, and grinned. She returned a plastic smile. "Let's make a deal," she said, her tone cutting but measured. "If you don't waste my time, I won't waste yours. We all understand you have an important mission—building AI robots and contributing to the Great Leader's peaceful objectives. But first, this interview. The people need to know they can trust you. You must answer all the questions. Deal?"

Elmo's smile broadened into a laugh. "Deal," he replied with a chuckle. He leaned back on the couch, ready to engage.

The interviewer pressed forward, "How do you feel about betraying the United States with your allegiance to the North Korean Communist Party?"

The pointed question didn't shake Elmo. "My allegiance," he began calmly, "is to the honest pursuit of positive progress—nothing more, nothing less. Not to a country, not to a nationality, and not to a political creed. When I reach a crossroads, whether it's a major decision or a small one, I choose the path that leads to more truth."

He paused, his gaze steady. "I didn't betray the United States. And anyone who says I did is uneducated about history or pushing their own agenda. Let's be honest: the loudest voices calling me a traitor belong to those who've lost the profits gained by preventing the Korean people from determining their own destiny."

The interviewer raised an eyebrow and leaned slightly forward. "So, you want the Korean people to be free and prosper?"

Elmo replied, "Yes, of course. I also want that for the people of the United States. As long as no one uses their freedom and prosperity to oppress the truth and make profits off the propagation of lies."

The interviewer said, "You talk so much about the truth, but many believe you've hidden your real background. Many believe you were a CIA agent, not in the Army. Are you a hypocrite? A fraud? Why should anyone trust you?"

Elmo burst into laughter, slapped his knee a few times, then gathered himself. "CIA? No, definitely not. I applied to the agency a long time ago and failed their interview process. As you know, they do very thorough background checks. Not as thorough as North Korea, but still. After I failed their full-scope polygraph, the CIA told me plainly they didn't have a place for a late age bedwetter with unresolved daddy and mommy issues. North Korea knows I wasn't with the CIA because they obtained copies of the files the CIA and NSA have on me. If North Korea knows my background and trusts me, why shouldn't anyone else? Hypocrite? No. Fraud? No."

The interviewer leaned in closer and rested a hand gently on Elmo's knee. "Just to be clear," she said with a faint smile, "I'm not calling you a fraud, Elmo. Every interaction I've had with you convinces me you're just a simple scientist who is now… in love?"

Elmo bit his lip with a bashful smile and shook his head. He laughed nervously before he answered, "Sora and I… Sora. I don't have words yet for what Sora is to me."

The interviewer didn't let Elmo off the hook with a follow-up question. She leaned in and waited for him to elaborate.

Elmo's eyes wandered past the lights and cameras, and focused on the scientists who trickled into the lab for the morning work call.

The North Korean Barbara Walters tried to draw his attention back to the interview. "That's Dr. Michaelson. Mind always on his work. That's another question we're all dying to know the answer to. How does Sora fit into your AI project?"

Elmo's gaze shifted and locked onto Sora as she sat gracefully in her makeup chair, surrounded by a flurry of busy hands. She wore a simple gray Korean hanbok, the kind often worn by monks. The understated outfit highlighted her abundant natural beauty.

Their eyes met across the room. Elmo stood up from the interview couch, stepped carefully over all the cords, and wove his way through the production crew.

From her director's chair, Kim Yeo Jeong clenched her jaw, clasped her hands in front of her, leaned forward, and furrowed her brow in concentration, as though she confronted a math problem finally complex enough to demand her full focus.

Elmo reached Sora's makeup chair and gently took her hand in his. She stood in front of him, blushed, and radiated joy. Elmo twirled her around. He couldn't breathe. Didn't need to breathe.

The two dogs howled from their cages. The scruffy

mutt and the Shiba, both penned up after long journeys, were restless. Their noses twitched, filled with each other's pheromones. They were both ready to burst through the doors of their cages.

Hand in hand, Elmo and Sora walked over to Old Dr. Jeong, who stood by the kennels and looked exasperated. Elmo motioned for him to release the dogs. With a reluctant sigh, Dr. Jeong opened the cages.

The Shiba and the mutt skipped butt-sniffing introductions and got right into doggy-style humping.

The mutt finished but wanted another round to make sure he planted every seed from his sack. However, the bitch knew she was the most fertile valley the mutt had ever had, or would ever have, so she was confident the seed took. When the mutt tried to mount the bitch again, she snapped her head back and bit the mutt. The mutt didn't mind getting bit. In fact, he interpreted this as a sign to pump and grind a little harder.

When the Shiba let out a startled yelp, Sora's reaction was swift and commanding. She barked—a loud, piercing sound that echoed across the lab. The room fell silent, and every head turned toward her in stunned curiosity.

The mutt responded to Sora's alpha female command bark by immediately going flaccid and dismounted the Shiba. Both dogs settled next to each other on the floor. No hard feelings. They gave each other space to lick their respective genitals clean.

Sora looked at Elmo, who was flabbergasted. Sora kissed him on the cheek. She took a knee next to the dogs, who paused from their respective crotches to give doggy smiling acknowledgements to their alpha queen Sora.

Old Dr. Jeong leaned toward Elmo and asked, "Is. Is. Thaw, thaw, thaw. That. That Kah kah Kim? Is that Kim Yeo Jeong?"

Elmo remembered the interview. He turned back toward the cameras while Kim Yeo Jeong marched purposefully in his direction, her index finger sliced through the air with silent commands that clearly translated to, "stay calm and press onward."

Meanwhile, Sora turned to Old Dr. Jeong and asked, "Do you have names for the dogs?"

Old Dr. Jeong shook his head and responded, "Nah. Nah. No names. From rough backgrounds. Nah. Nah. Not nice pounds."

Elmo followed Kim Yeo Jeong's cue to stay natural and remained with Sora and the dogs. The mutt finished licking himself clean, eagerly bounded over to Elmo, and initiated a playful wrestling match.

Elmo handled the slobbering mutt with a head lock-belly rub combination. The mutt's eyes drooped and his tongue lolled out in pure bliss. Elmo made sure he got a full submission from the dog and asked, "Who's a good boy? Huh? Who's a good boy?"

Elmo kept his WWE move in action and said

to Sora, "This one is Barklee. We're calling the male Barklee."

The Shiba, not to be outdone, scooted over to Sora and nuzzled against her. Sora smiled and gave the dog soft, soothing ear rubs.

While he still rubbed Barklee's belly, Elmo glanced over and asked, "What do we call the Shiba?"

Sora looked down at the dog and then toward the cameras. A flicker of relief crossed her face as she realized how much Elmo loved dogs, too. She paused to let the moment settle before she replied, "Daisuki."

The interviewer caught the cinematic tension. She dropped to one knee beside them and asked Sora in a soft voice, "How do you feel about Elmo?"

Sora turned to the interviewer and repeated firmly, "Daisuki."

Elmo overheard her and attempted to mimic the Japanese word without understanding it. "Daisuki," he repeated, then grinned as if suddenly convinced. "Daisuki. Of course. It couldn't be anything else."

Sora gave the cameras a cheeky, knowing smile, her expression full of mischief and charm.

From her director's chair, Kim Yeo Jeong let the scene linger just long enough to maximize the emotional weight before she finally barked, "Cut!"

The mutt and Elmo knew it was time to let the belly rub rest before chaffing could set in and ruin the next opportunity. Elmo stood up. The mutt licked his hands with big thank you laps.

Kim Yeo Jeong gave Elmo a curt nod. "Your interview is complete. Go do your science mission."

Elmo didn't need to be told twice. With a quick glance at Sora and a determined stride, he left the set and rejoined his team, ready to dive back into science.

17

Sora stayed with the dogs, not playing fetch or rubbing their bellies, but making noises that sounded unmistakably like dog communication. Kim Yeo Jeong signaled to the camera crew and the North Korean Barbara Walters to resume the interview.

This was the big moment. Sora's past was a mystery to the world; she had seemingly come from nowhere when she became a star. Famously private, she had never submitted to an interview or revealed any personal details to the public. Even North Korea's intelligence service had been unable to find her official records during their background check.

The interviewer asked, "Sora, what exactly are you doing with the dogs?"

Sora replied casually, "Talking to them. I can talk to animals sometimes—but with dogs, almost all the time."

As soon as the words left her mouth, Sora's shoulders tensed, her chest caved slightly, and she winced. Through squinted eyes, she glanced across the room at

Elmo, who orchestrated his team. The lab coats moved with buoyant energy, smiled, and even whistled as they worked. Sora probed her thoughts and realized she didn't feel ashamed or stupid about what she had just said. Her rigid pose melted, and she sank back into an easy, flowing form.

The interviewer asked a follow-up, "Wait, did you say you can communicate with dogs and other animals?"

Sora continued, "Yes, I realized I could talk to dogs and some other animals about the same time I got into pornography."

The interviewer's eyes widened, and her nostrils flared subtly with each measured breath. She leaned forward, draped her jagged judgments in a veil of polite silk, and said, "Oh, how nice. Very interesting. Please, tell me more."

Sora stopped her dog noises and focused her gaze with newfound determination. She stroked the Shiba's head rhythmically, and said, "I wasn't the only one, you know. The girls who got duped… it's all connected, I guess. Well, anyway, I'll tell you. I'll finally tell the world."

She let out a sharp, angry laugh and continued, "The story everyone's been waiting to hear: how Sora Aoi— 'the Fountain of Youth'—ended up in pornography."

Sora began her story, explained that it all started during a solo trip to South Korea on her summer break from college. She had it all planned out: stay in a youth hostel, eat kimbap, and take K-pop dance classes. She wanted to get all the youthful exuberance out of her system before she finished her degree in accounting and became a serious adult.

However, her entire plan went out the window after only a week of dance classes. A talent scout approached her after class—polished in a three-button suit and sported an Omega watch. He made an irresistible offer: skip dinner with the other students and ride across town in his Rolls Royce to discuss her potential as a K-pop star. "At the very least," he assured her, "you could land a gig as a backup dancer before heading back to university."

It was easy to say yes. Over the next two weeks, the talent scout devoted himself to her, arranged meetings with modeling agencies, and secured auditions for real K-pop training programs. He swept Sora up in the whirlwind and convinced her that her dreams were within reach.

But after those two weeks of relentless effort, there were no offers. The scout delivered the feedback with a regretful smile: "Everyone sees your raw talent, but there's one consistent issue. They won't consider you unless you've got at least C-cup boobs."

The talent scout made plastic surgery seem like a straightforward decision for Sora. He explained the procedure would essentially pay for itself with a modeling contract so lucrative, her first two paychecks would more than cover the medical expenses. The deal sounded too good to pass up. To ensure she didn't leave for another agency after her "beautification," the scout persuaded her to let him hold on to her passport until she fulfilled the contract.

After she sealed the arrangement, the scout handed Sora off to another set of handlers. They assured her it would take about a month to arrange her first photoshoot, but in the meantime, they would take care of her every need. They provided her with a brand-new cellphone, designer clothes, high-end diet consultations, and a modern one-room apartment in downtown Gangnam, where several other model recruits also lived.

The surgery came quickly, and afterward, Sora stayed in her apartment to recover and allow time for the swelling and bruising to heal before she ventured out. As she rested and adjusted to her new life, she explored the hallways of the apartment. She quickly noticed something strange: the other recruits, who lived in the rooms next to hers, avoided her. When she tried to introduce herself, they barely made eye contact, their reluctance palpable and unsettling.

Kim Yeo Jeong couldn't believe that all came out. It was better than anything she anticipated. Her mind raced with calculations until it settled on a firm belief that the unexpected turn wouldn't disappoint her brother. She leaned forward in her chair and anxiously observed the interviewer, who wisely allowed Sora to continue her monologue uninterrupted.

Sora explained how blindsided she felt when they canceled her first photoshoot. Instead of a promising start to her modeling career, they gave her crushing news: she was still obligated to make the first payment on her plastic surgery debt. To make matters worse, all the luxury items they'd provided—the cellphone, designer clothes, diet consultations—weren't gifts but lifestyle expenses they expected her to cover. The costs had ballooned her debt to over $45,000 in just one month.

"I couldn't call my parents for help," Sora said bitterly. "Not with Mom in Finland, living her new life with my stepdad. And Dad? On some street somewhere drunk by noon every day."

Her handlers, however, presented a way out. A smaller gig was available, they said, but it came with a condition: she'd need to pose nude, with particular emphasis on her vagina. Desperate and out of options, Sora reluctantly agreed.

After the shoot, she felt filthy. She sat in the dressing room, hastily pulled on her clothes, and wrestled with an overwhelming sense of shame. Before she could process it all, her handlers barged in without knocking. They flaunted the thin stack of bills she'd earned, only to inform her that every cent would go straight toward her debt.

She hadn't even finished dressing when the man she later came to know as her contract manager entered unannounced. He started with compliments, praised her work and her body. Without warning, he sidled up behind her and massaged her shoulders. The compliments grew more suggestive. Then he kissed her.

Sora pulled away and asked him to stop. He didn't.

He shoved her to the floor and raped her.

Sora's voice broke as she recounted the events. For a moment, she stared into the distance, her expression unreadable. Then a venomous rage washed over her face. Through gritted teeth, she growled her next words.

"I didn't fight back. I didn't scream. No!"

She paused and closed her eyes as tears streamed down her cheeks. Her voice dropped to a whisper, and she trembled with sobs. "No. I thrust my hips and begged him to finish. To get it over with faster."

Sora wiped her tears away with the sleeves of her hanbok. She inhaled deeply to steady herself. Her expression hardened as she activated the mental defense mechanism she'd relied on countless times before—a cold, robotic compartmentalization that allowed her to navigate life while she pretended everything was fine. That there wasn't a gaping, festering wound in her soul.

When she spoke again, her tone was flat, matter-of-fact. "I locked that memory away a long time ago. I hate myself for bringing it out now. But not as much as I hate myself for being so weak and stupid."

She described how she laid there on the carpet, numb, and stared at the ceiling as he zipped up his pants. The manager loomed over her and smiled as if he had done her a favor. Then he reached into his wallet and pulled out five crisp hundred-dollar bills.

" 'Here,' he said, and waved the money in front of me. 'This will help pay off your debt.' "

Sora didn't shower until her minders had dragged her back up to her apartment and into her room. Once alone, she spent hours scrubbing herself raw until there were patches of bloody skin in places on her body.

Eventually, she wandered into the apartment's communal kitchen. The cupboards held nothing appetizing. She poured herself a bowl of American cereal—some frosted junk—and sat at the table. With mechanical motions, she scooped up spoonfuls, only to dump them back into the bowl. Soon, the cereal dissolved into a soggy, uneaten mush. Sora stared blankly into the distance, her mind a fog, until…

A little mutt padded over and nuzzled against her leg.

She kicked the dog away.

The motion startled her. It wasn't like her—not like her at all. Someone else had done that, someone inhabiting her body.

It didn't faze the mutt. He backed off for a moment, then approached again, more cautiously, and stopped a few feet away. His dark, round eyes looked up at her with a mix of curiosity and sadness.

Then, something impossible happened.

The dog introduced himself as Franklin. He said he was used to getting kicked. His voice, though hesitant, carried an apologetic tone. "I don't speak Korean very well," Franklin had explained. "I'm not a Korean dog."

Franklin apologized for touching Sora without permission and added, "I understand why you're upset. I'm so sorry this happened to you. I wish you'd never had to experience such cruelty." He hesitated, then continued, "I can't begin to imagine what you're going through, but… you're not alone. The other girls here—they've been through very similar things."

Sora explained that she and Franklin, the dog, communicated subliminally. Most of the time, she didn't need to exchange sounds with a dog to understand them. However, on occasion, a bark or growl helped clarify a thought or amplify a message beyond the limits of nonverbal communication. She likened her connection with dogs to a radio transmission, where they'd broadcast thoughts and feelings back and forth. It had taken her years to translate the transmissions into a human language with any fluency.

Franklin told Sora he was surprised she could understand him. He'd never encountered a human who could speak their secret dog language so well.

He was blunt and asked her if she wanted his help to get out of this situation before she became a sex slave.

Sora didn't know how to respond to Franklin. He interpreted her silence to be a quiet, desperate "yes."

Franklin explained to Sora that the manager would come to the apartment the next day at 8:00 a.m. to present her with a onetime opportunity. It wouldn't be much of an improvement in the short term, but it could lead to true happiness—maybe.

He said the manager would bring some women from the brothel he ran and suggested she seize the chance. Franklin then shared his philosophy, and claimed dogs have a special power to guide humans back onto the right track, as long as they listened and understood one thing: it's necessary to pass through hell before reaching heaven. "That's a universal rule," he said.

Most humans, he continued, remained stuck in hell because they refused to embrace suffering and let the pain burn a lesson of wisdom into their soul. Franklin was often preachy and used the moment to elaborate on what he thought was missing from the story of Jesus—what He endured during His three days in hell.

According to Franklin, Jesus faced every torment the demons could throw at Him, laughed in their faces, and dared them to do more. "What happened on earth was just the tip of the iceberg," Franklin explained. "The key to Jesus's escape was His ability to feed off pain. Eventually, the demons lost heart—they couldn't torture Him anymore."

He concluded with advice for Sora: "Don't complain about this life. Don't blame others. Embrace your struggles. In the end, you'll meet the love of your life and find true happiness, true contentment."

Franklin instructed Sora to approach the manager when he arrived and ask for a job at the brothel to pay off her debt. "Ask to start immediately," he said, and promised the manager would agree.

Sora followed Franklin's guidance, approached the manager, and asked if she could work as one of his prostitutes. As Franklin predicted, the manager agreed to give her a chance.

Sora rode in a black van with the other women to the brothel that night. In a run-down dressing room no one had cleaned or remodeled in decades, the women changed clothes and applied thick layers of makeup.

Sora had followed Franklin's advice to the letter, and jotted it down as he explained it to her in the kitchen. She had ripped open a cereal box and used a pen to write on the inside surface. "I still have those notes in my keepsake chest back in Japan," she said.

Her first night at the brothel began around 9:00 p.m. Sora joined a line of women, all dressed in school-girl uniforms—similar in theme, but each slightly different.

"We walked into a dimly lit room," Sora recounted, "where a group of businessmen waited to choose a girl to fuck. I'm sorry for the language, but with prostitu-tion, the only appropriate word is 'fuck.' It's not sex, it's not making love, and it's not really rape—not in most cases, at least. It's just fucking."

Sora followed Franklin's advice and focused on the man at the center of the group—a short, shriveled, deeply scarred figure who appeared well over eighty. "He was well-dressed but very ugly. And old as dirt," Sora said. She'd caught his eye and winked at him.

Unsurprisingly, the man chose her.

Once in the room, Sora placed her purse in the corner. She'd cut a hole in it, with her phone's camera duct-taped inside, aimed at the bed. The old man paid her no attention, busy undressing and neatly hanging up his clothes.

"When he laid down, flaccid and covered in liver spots, he looked like a naked Mr. Burns from *The Simpsons*," Sora remarked. "I don't know what he expected. Actually, I do. He expected the usual: a transactional fuck. Nothing more, nothing less. But Franklin had instructed me to do something different—something the old man wouldn't expect."

Standing beside the bed, Sora began the ritual Franklin had described. She hovered her hands millimeters above his body and brushed the peach fuzz on his skin. Slowly, she worked her way up from his feet and ignored his whiskey-soaked breath and dozed off demeanor.

"When I reached his nipples, he stirred. By the time I got to his lips, he was semi-conscious, maybe thirty percent awake," she explained.

Sora discreetly pulled out the cardboard with Franklin's instructions to prepare for the next step. She put a condom on her finger, added lube, and squirted a bit of minty fresh mouthwash onto the tip. Then, following Franklin's method, she gently circled the old man's anus and applied light pressure.

He jolted awake as her finger entered and stimulated his prostate. Almost immediately, the old man responded, and got as hard as a raging teenage boy.

"Some people think you can skip the hand-hover routine and jump straight to anal play," Sora explained. "They're wrong. And you can't do the hover without fully focusing your mind on the body beneath your hands. It's about priming the subject—giving care to their physical form."

She reflected. "You don't need to love the person—they're often liars, cheats, greedy, and despicable. But you must love the beastly animal form in front of you. That's the key. Not love as in passion—it's dangerous to let their emotions reach you. You must build a wall around your heart. That is the key to protect yourself. But to care for the beastly body? That you must do. And that's easy, because the animal part is at least honest. Anyway."

Sora snorted a laugh before she continued, "Where was I? Oh yeah, the old man was awake and hard as a rock. He was so shocked by his boner he just laid there and let me work. With one finger up his ass, I used my free hand to jerk him off. I timed the strokes to complement the undulating pressure I applied to the walls of his anus.

"I followed Franklin's instructions exactly and rocked my body in a rhythm I learned in a dance class—the one that brought me to South Korea in the first place. I synced my movements to the beat of a techno song called 'Moon' by Kid Francescoli. Franklin knew my heart. He knew how much I loved that song, so it always played in my head."

Sora's smile faded as she stared off into the distance before she continued to tell the interviewer her story. "I couldn't let the old man inside me—not my anus, not my vagina, not my mouth. I wasn't ready for that. Besides, my vagina was still raw from being raped the day before by the South Korean pimp. Lucky for me, he had a tiny penis. This old man, though? It took less than five minutes of my routine before he shot a rocket of a load that hit the ceiling.

"Just as Franklin advised, I drank so much water before I left that day. I held my bladder for hours. By the time I got into the lineup, I couldn't think about anything else, but nerves and—well, excitement— helped me hold it in.

"When the old man came, he had a heart attack. The cell phone camera caught it all—him convulsing and me convulsing in perfect sync. Right after his cum shot up to the ceiling, I timed it. I climbed on top of him, rubbed my beaver on his belly, and urinated all over him. But the way it looked on camera, it seemed like I sprayed him with an orgasm. It's unbelievable how well a phone camera can shoot a scene, even back then. The footage was perfect.

"When it was over, I laid my head on his chest.

And since I was completely exhausted, it looked like I was genuinely satisfied. But almost immediately, I realized his heart wasn't beating. Maybe. I don't know. I still don't know, I just remember feeling relief. The look on his face was pure ecstasy. He died happy."

Sora continued, "About thirty minutes later, the manager called the phone in the room to ask if the session was done, if the old man was dressed and ready to leave, and if there were any problems. I told him the old man had fallen asleep and suggested someone come wake him.

"At a place like that, you can't call an ambulance. They carried the old man out and took him somewhere for someone to find him dead in a way that wouldn't ruin his family's memory of him.

The scene. All the chaos that followed. The rest of the night, they closed the brothel for business. They took all us ladies back to the apartment. I went straight to my room, where Franklin waited. He sat on my lap and walked me through basic video editing on my phone. I was surprised how well he knew the software.

"When the video was ready, I uploaded the full version online along with a teaser trailer. I set up a pay site, which wasn't common back then. Sure, there were free sites, but nothing with clickbait trailers like mine."

Sora sighed. "It turned out the manager who raped me got into some big trouble. As everyone knows, they never arrest people for prostitution in South Korea, but he got arrested. It turned out the manager didn't handle the old man's death properly. The authorities also didn't follow normal protocol either, because the police didn't tip anyone off when they planned the arrest. So, when the raid happened, the manager and all his pimp aids were eating noodles in the back room of the brothel. The bust was all over the news. The old man who died? He was a National Assembly member, and the younger men with him were real estate developers who sought his help with legislation. Something like building high-rise apartments on one of the US Army's vacated military bases in Seoul."

Sora paused. "The pimps only got a few years in jail. Of course, they weren't charged with rape, though I wasn't their only victim. But with them gone, my debt disappeared.

"So I was free, just like that, but I also didn't have any spending money, a passport, or any place to go. I stayed in the apartment and no one showed up to kick me out. So, I hunkered down and ran my porn website, which earned me a few thousand dollars a week. And, before I knew it, I had enough money to find my way out of South Korea.

"I also had a new skill. I could stroke old men off with an expert technique. Give them the best orgasm of their life. Give them a happy ending. Spray them with urine. I became Sora Aoi, the Fountain of Youth. That schoolgirl outfit. The first scene I ever did. You'd be surprised how much power a young woman can access if she has a psychic dog helping her get to the right nightclubs at the right time to meet old men looking for a heart-stopping orgasm. It didn't take long for me to meet the right people who got me the documents I needed to get to Japan."

Her tone softened. "Of course, I brought Franklin with me when I finally left South Korea. He was the best boy ever. He talked me through my early years and helped me become a huge porn star. Franklin helped me decide which roles to take. Which agent to hire. Representatives who wouldn't try to be my pimp.

"When Franklin died, I couldn't bring myself to get another dog. But I couldn't let my gift for talking with canines go to waste, so I became a weekend volunteer at the animal shelter near my apartment.

"The dogs were my escape, my peace. They seemed to sense something special coming my way before my trip to North Korea. None of them warned me about Elmo, though."

Sora smirked and continued. "Naturally, Elmo's request to meet me was shocking. He was still young enough, handsome, and a superstar. And I'm still surprised he hasn't asked me to pee on him yet."

As Sora finished, she stared into the distance and looked like a soldier caught between the horrors of the past and the safety of the present.

Kim Yeo Jeong had experience consoling people through PTSD. After all, she was there for her brother when he executed their favorite uncle. Kim Yeo Jeong motioned to the interviewer to give Sora space. Kim

Yeo Jeong kept the cameras rolling and knew it's best to sit close, not say anything, and be ready for any explosive emotion to come out at any moment. It could be mad laughter, uncontrollable sobbing, anything.

The two dogs cuddled up close to Sora and whimpered. Sora joined them. The dogs licked her hands. Used their wet noses to pry open a small space for their heads to wiggle under her arms. Sora was lovingly mashed between the two-dog team. When her whimpering subsided, she excused herself and left the lab with the dogs close by her side. The camera crew followed a comfortable distance behind.

Once out in the sunlight, Sora sat on the lawn and picked dandelions. She popped off the heads of the younger flowers and blew seeds from the mature ones without making wishes.

Sora stayed out on the lawn in front of the lab like that for the rest of the day. She moved to a new spot when she needed to find a fresh dandelion population. Grounded by the quiet companionship of her dogs.

18

SORA'S MONOLOGUE CAST a cloud of intoxicating introspection on the entire film crew except for Kim Yeo Jeong, who took a second in her director's chair while her eyes darted around the room as she calculated all the opportunities that had only just become possible. She stood, brushed the dust off her pants suit, and marched outside to the production van.

Kim Yeo Jeong took a snort of meth before she climbed in beside her technicians. While she stood over their shoulders, she orchestrated a breakneck pace of edits and effects.

In less than eight hours, the crew had produced a rough cut of the interview and three supplemental propaganda-style episodes. Kim Yeo Jeong leveraged her access to state video archives and seamlessly spliced in key footage to enhance the narrative. She used security tapes of Sora and Elmo's first meeting at the ballroom—carefully edited to omit the violence—and scenes from their first night at Elmo's house, with all explicit content removed.

The production crafted by Kim Yeo Jeong was a rollercoaster of golden television. It masterfully wove Elmo and Sora's backstories into a compelling narrative arc that culminated in Sora's raw and hard-hitting account of rape, human trafficking, and her delusional belief in her ability to communicate with animals.

A stunning soundtrack tied the entire production together and elevated further the episodes.

(Note from Eric Palmateer to his editors: Fuck you. I won't explain what I mean by stunning. Just believe me, it was better than you can imagine. Even if you can imagine something pretty awesome, Kim Yeo Jeong's production was better than that. So, fuck you. It was amazing.)

Kim Yeo Jeong carried the tape to her sedan parked nearby. She settled into the back seat, inserted the interview into the onboard computer, and picked up her encrypted satellite phone capable of connecting her to anyone in the North Korean Party, including her brother.

The Great Leader was a little surprised and very annoyed when he saw his sister's call. She knew his schedule; that's why she knew to call the phone on his private airplane. He was already halfway to Paris for the most important international summit in the history of the world.

"I have the ultimate weapon for you, brother! You can finally crush our enemies and ensure we're remembered as the ultimate good guys in the eternal history books," she said.

The Great Leader heard *ultimate weapon* and *crush our enemies* and his brain put his annoyance on pause. "I'm listening…" he replied.

The Great Leader approved his sister's plan and granted her full authority to use state intelligence to investigate Sora's claims about young Asian women being coerced into prostitution in South Korea. However, then he reminded his sister he was very busy and didn't want to be bothered with any more details. "Just get it done. And don't make any more mistakes," he barked at her before hanging up.

Kim Yeo Jeong wasted no time. She immediately made more calls.

First, she summoned the top construction official in Pyongyang to the lab. "Bring your best people tomorrow morning," she ordered. When he asked for details, she curtly replied, "You'll be briefed on-site."

Next, she contacted the deputy of the State Security Department. Within minutes, cell phone records, bank account details, criminal network analyses, and other data on South Korean nationals involved in sex trafficking flooded her inbox. They already tracked the intelligence, so it was simply a matter of organizing and disseminating the files to her.

She didn't stop there. Kim Yeo Jeong also requested an unbiased comparative analysis to show South Korean private corporations as world leaders in the international sex trade—a recurring requirement for state security to measure North Korea's own relative position in the sex slave market. Those reports arrived just as quickly.

She skipped lunch and maintained her energy with small doses of meth, laser-focused on delivering results. Her next step was to pitch the project to Netflix. She envisioned a two-step release strategy: first, the interview and background story, then a salacious intelligence report distributed to media outlets worldwide.

With her temporary authority, she instructed North Korea's elite hackers to stand by, ready to deploy aggressive clickbait strategies to amplify global attention on the interview, Sora's story, and the damning intelligence report.

The media executives at Netflix were stunned—not only by the speed of the delivery, but by the sheer quality of the material. They quickly bought into the release strategy and, more importantly, Kim Yeo Jeong's vision and execution captivated them.

Running on days without sleep, Kim Yeo Jeong knew better than to push beyond her doctor-prescribed meth limits. She delegated operations to a small, trusted team who could stall any major decisions for the next forty-eight hours.

Finally, she stepped back for some much-needed downtime. Her plans included blood transfusions from pubescent female virgins, cryotherapy treatments, and, most importantly, a well-deserved rest.

Kim Yeo Jeong wasn't the only one who needed

recovery time. After a long day at the lab, Elmo found Sora on the completely dandelion-free lawn. She leaned into his arms, and he held her as they walked home. He didn't ask about the confessions she'd made during her interview, and she didn't volunteer any details.

The lab's designated space for the dogs had become the interview setup, and left the Shiba and the mutt without a proper home. Elmo solved the problem and declared the dogs would stay at the lab during the day for study, and come home with him and Sora at night.

That evening, Sora barely touched her grilled fish and miso soup. She didn't say a word to Elmo either, only breaking out of her empty stare a few times to look down and pet the dogs, who refused to leave her side.

Elmo didn't pretend to understand what Sora went through. When Sora snuggled up into bed, Elmo tucked her in, but he didn't get under the covers with her. Instead, he brought a chair from the living room and placed it beside the bed. He sat there all night, with the dogs sleeping at his feet, and listened to his heartbeat dance along with his breath.

A few times, Elmo stood over Sora and softly brushed the hair on her sleeping head. He wanted to kiss Sora's forehead softly, but he knew it wasn't the night for that.

He nodded off a few times, but he was always there, a steady, calm presence. Each time Sora woke from her tossing and turning, she saw him there in the dark. The knowledge Elmo was there, a guardian in the waking world, gave Sora what she needed to go back into a deep sleep and face down her demons.

The next morning, she felt like Muhammad Ali after the Rumble in the Jungle, victorious but beaten to shit. She perked up a few times when she saw Elmo enjoying the coffee she'd made for him, but she did not forcibly hold on to a smile or pretend everything was okay.

As they walked hand in hand to the lab, the dogs darted ahead, circled back, and wove around them until they reached the grounds. There, construction trucks mingled with media vans.

A production staff member ran out and greeted Sora on the lawn in front of the lab. They had Sora's agent on the cell phone. Sora held the phone on speaker so Elmo could hear.

Her agent delivered the news: Netflix had decided not to revise the interview Kim Yeo Jeong had sent. Recognizing the five second collective global attention span, they'd already made the video available for streaming to capitalize on the momentum of Sora's viral fame.

The strategy worked beyond anyone's expectations. So many people streamed the video that some countries suspended civilian internet services to preserve bandwidth for critical infrastructure, like hospitals and water treatment facilities.

Hearing that, Sora's bumps and bruises from the

rough night all disappeared. The mass of shame that always lived in her gut dissolved and floated away. She felt a sudden relief, no more struggling to stand up straight and tall. No more wasting energy hiding her vulnerabilities.

Elmo listened intently and rubbed the small of Sora's back while the good news flowed in. He knew better than to spoil Sora's moment. He didn't bring up his justified suspicion that the North Korean computer experts had set up a perfect series of delectable click bait breadcrumbs that made it damn near impossible to avoid accessing a Netflix subscription to watch the interview.

When Sora kissed him on the cheek, it was his cue to leave for the lab. As he walked away, he thrust his fist into the air exuberantly and shouted, "Yes!" like he was an NBA announcer rejoicing a buzzer-beating three-pointer.

Sora smiled at his silliness, then turned her attention to business. She hung up the call, gave the dogs a good scruffy pet, and stepped into her new confident clean future.

The lab grounds buzzed. Teams of North Korean officials lined up and cameras rolled as Kim Yeo Jeong's staff explained the new direction for Sora's show. Titled *Doggy Style with Sora Aoi*, the program would feature her playing with dogs, training them, designing outfits, and interpreting their "communication" on camera.

Even though it was essentially a theme-based reality

show, they still had to do makeup before the shoot, and Sora used the opportunity to make a diva-like demand: she wanted to wear a dog-themed costume instead of traditional Korean attire. With Kim Yeo Jeong still in recovery, the officials reluctantly agreed and figured Sora could take the blame if there were any issues.

Dressed in a onesie, pajama-style doggy outfit, complete with ears and a small brown dot painted on her nose, Sora stood before the cameras. With the Shiba and mutt at her side, she directed North Korea's top engineers on how to create a doggy paradise. She frequently "consulted" the dogs for their input, before she explained anything to the construction team.

A week later, the paradise was complete. The sprawling three-story structure overshadowed the lab with its slides, ropes, ball pits, chew rooms, and a network of cameras and microphones. The production team monitored everything, instead of state security analysts.

Kim Yeo Jeong rose from her Lazarus-like treatment and approved of everything going on. Kim Yeo Jeong worked mostly from the vans parked in front of the lab. She stood over her technicians' shoulders, condensed the week's events into three episodes, which Netflix streamed immediately. The demand for Sora's content was so intense that several countries brokered emergency agreements with Netflix to air the show on national broadcast frequencies.

Meanwhile, Kim Yeo Jeong used her temporary

authority to release damning intelligence to link South Korean corporations to international sex trafficking. She knew it might require prayers for forgiveness later, but she was confident her brother would reward her boldness.

19

In Paris, the Great Leader stood among the world's most powerful leaders and discussed climate change accords when the Netflix interview released. He opened the summit by publicly downplaying his peace missile supremacy while securing agreements from every major leader to invest in North Korea's plan to become a carbon-neutral nation. The World Bank granted an unprecedented $100 billion zero-interest loan, and top universities worldwide pledged to collaborate with North Korea as a test bed for state-run, fossil-free transportation systems.

The Great Leader achieved everything he wanted within the first few days of the summit.

Then, the release of the intelligence report changed everything. The damning revelations about South Korea's sex trafficking industry shocked the world. With cameras rolling, the Great Leader expertly leveraged the moment and presented himself as a crusader for justice. He demanded a united global front to address South Korea's heinous deeds and declared that unification talks could not proceed until South Korea verifiably ended their human rights abuses.

He could hardly believe how quickly his sister had delivered this opportunity. While outwardly solemn, he struggled to conceal his jubilation. Of course, he'd shower Kim Yeo Jeong with blessings later—but for the moment, there were victories to claim.

"The only rightful course of action," the Great Leader declared, "is for North Korea—the trustworthy Korea—to be the place where South Korea repays its debt to the women of Asia."

The world's leaders, spellbound by his rhetoric, unanimously agreed. It was decided: an international women's school would be established in North Korea. Underprivileged young women from around the globe would receive full scholarships, funded by South Korea, to study from primary school through a Ph.D. in Juche Studies at Kim Il Sung University.

With this triumph, the Great Leader was free to spend the remaining weeks of the summit on a victory lap. He had it all: the ultimate weapon in the EMP missile, the world building his carbon-free infrastructure, the top-rated television show, the retreat of American forces from his peninsula, and global recognition as the good guy.

The only thing that could screw up all the Great Leader's success was a round of self-destructive behavior. He had only one vice powerful enough to destroy his victory. An old foe he'd never learned how to master.

And what always brought him down? A gout attack. And what triggered his gout attacks? His best friend, greatest love, and worst enemy, Toblerone chocolate.

The love affair started back when he was at Swiss boarding school. Whenever he was at his highest or lowest, only one thing could make the moment right. He found the only way to get everything he needed out of his chocolate lover was to pack his mouth full of it, then use one hand covered in melted chocolate to masturbate and use his other hand to give himself anal pleasure with a frozen bar of the chocolate.

Yet Toblerone was a jealous lover. If it found whiskey, red meat, or cheese in his system, it unleashed a nuclear war of gout attacks that left the Great Leader incapacitated.

The Great Leader's top security advisor, Minister Park, knew all about the Toblerone problem, but the minister had no desire to use the information against the Great Leader. Minister Park had dedicated his entire life to serving the Kim family. He even delayed getting justice for his youngest son's death so the Party could milk Elmo for AI technology. The Minister knew they would reward his loyalty when his oldest son, his pride and joy, the future of his family line, became a general in Kim Jeong Un's Army.

Minister Park knew the summit meetings would inundate Kim Jeong Un with too much excitement, too much stress, so the minister made certain all rooms were clean of Toblerone or any similar chocolates.

Minister Park knew it was imperative that the Great Leader didn't even smell the Toblerone, in any of its forms. Even just a glob on someone's chin, ten feet away, and the Great Leader could blood hound smell that shit. And, if he was way past tired and stressed and he smelled that delicious devil chocolate, then the Great Leader would turn into a werewolf mother fucking motherfucker and tear everything down to get that chocolate into his mouth.

Minister Park knew he must ensure, at all costs, that Kim Jeong Un didn't have to face any Toblerone temptation until the trip was over and he was back in North Korea and fully recovered from all the excitement of becoming the world's greatest leader.

20

THE GREAT LEADER, like his father and grandfather before him, relied on the ultimate insurance policy: the country's secret police and intelligence apparatus.

The ruling Kim family had established clear, non-negotiable priorities for the forces to ensure the North Korean Communist Party never faced the threat of an uprising. Their first and foremost priority was the survival of the Great Leader. The second was to monitor international activity for any potential threats to the regime, and analyze the intentions of every foreign person or organization that directed their attention toward North Korea. The third was surveilling domestic activity to identify and suppress dissident mindsets.

With Kim Jong Un traveling abroad and engaging with world leaders, the security forces were stretched thin and struggled to meet their primary mission. While they still ensured the Great Leader's safety, they had virtually no bandwidth left to monitor international activities for threats. The explosion of global attention on North Korea further overwhelmed their resources, making the second priority unattainable.

As a result, there were no resources left to surveil the North Korean populace. If any citizens with dissident leanings realized the regime's watchful eye—their "Eye of Sauron"—was momentarily averted, they'd see it as the perfect opportunity to plot against the state.

Luckily for the Great Leader, everyone loved and feared him, so he was safe from threats, both foreign and domestic.

21

IN THE LAB, Elmo was finally ready to take a leap and give his team the autonomy they needed to reach the next level. He would step back from the day-to-day grind.

While many respected Elmo as a visionary, manager, and motivator, few would consider him an elite mathematician. He had long accepted that when it came to high-level physics or engineering challenges, he wasn't the one to rely on for precise technical solutions. If his calculations had to serve as the foundation for critical decisions, the margin for error would likely be too high to proceed confidently.

With the lab set up for production and the camera crews occupied outside with Sora and her dogs, Elmo stood at the head of the round table in the conference room. He faced his team and laid down the challenge: they had four weeks to deliver a prototype for the robot dogs and demonstrate a beta test for the AI.

Those requirements punched the scientists in the gut. Four weeks. The timeline was suffocating. A few looked ready to complain, ask for guidance, or protest the impossibility of the task. But before anyone could speak up, Elmo cleared his throat and knocked his fist on the table three times to get the attention of everyone in his courtroom.

Elmo stood silent, and his presence filled the room. All eyes were on him. He didn't say a word.

Starting with the scientist to his right, Elmo made deliberate, unbroken eye contact with each person in turn, and moved around the table. As he looked into their eyes, he put his hands over his heart and focused on a specific moment when that individual had accomplished something brilliant—something pivotal to the team's success in developing the EMP missile.

One by one, the scientists felt the weight of his silent acknowledgment. The confidence they'd felt during their finest moments surged back to life. By the time Elmo had completed his silent circuit around the room, he'd convinced every person they could do *it*. Whatever *it* was, they'd find a way.

Rotund Dr. Cheong was an easy sell. Ever since he'd seen the idea pitched on a bootlegged copy of the *Lex Fridman Podcast*, he'd secretly dreamed of building a robot AI dog. He had already planned exactly how it could and should be done, so it thrilled him to take the lead on the project.

With everyone energized and on board, Elmo collapsed into his chair, drained from the emotional effort it had taken to connect with each individual on his team. A goofy smile spread across his face as he watched the scientists dive into the first steps of the scrum method. They buzzed with ideas, debated, decided, and covered the walls with sticky notes.

Without disrupting the group's momentum, Elmo quietly pulled Old Dr. Jeong aside.

"Can you get me a straw hat, a shovel, a hoe, and some chicken wire by tomorrow morning?" Elmo asked.

Old Dr. Jeong, who rarely needed to think twice about a request, replied, "Yah, yah, buh, buh, yah. Yeah, sure, but why?"

Elmo grinned. "I'm going to start a garden out behind the lab."

22

Outside the lab, everything Sora did with the dogs became footage for another instant hit. Kim Yeo Jeong and Netflix expanded the concept and created separate shows for each category of Sora's interactions with the dogs. One show featured Sora conferring with the dogs to create doggy fashion. Another showcased the dogs' insightful critiques on the taste, texture, and appearance of different dog foods. There was a training show, a playtime show, and even a program dedicated to doggy naps.

The results were staggering: the top ten Netflix shows all starred Sora and the dogs. The unprecedented popularity forced Netflix to overhaul its platform to create a dedicated *Doggy Style with Sora Aoi* channel separate from its regular dashboard.

Sora's original contract with Netflix covered only twenty episodes of content, which they quickly exhausted. The subsequent deal enabled the creation of these variety shows, but had been a challenge to negotiate. However, Sora smoothed the process and hired Kim Yeo Jeong as her new agent.

When the negotiations were complete, Sora's channel remained on Netflix but required viewers to pay an additional subscription fee. Kim Yeo Jeong, who understood the cultural and political significance of the project, ensured most of the profits would go toward her brother's new international initiative to educate young women in North Korea.

Netflix gained little from the deal except the exclusive rights to produce shows that analyzed and repackaged footage from Sora's channel. But that alone was enough. While the top ten programs on Netflix featured Sora and the dogs, the next tier of most-watched content consisted entirely of Netflix-exclusive shows that dissected, discussed, and celebrated Sora's antics with her canine companions.

· · ·

Next to the doggy paradise, Elmo spent his days working the land behind the lab. Though he could've used machinery to break the ground, he preferred to dig and hoe manually. He believed his sweat and effort were the key ingredients for his soil's fertilizer. Besides, there was no rush—his garden was for horseradish and garlic, a crop he wouldn't harvest until the next season.

Elmo had traded his lab coat for a more rustic look, complete with a farmer's tan in the spots not shaded by the huge, yellow straw hat he wore every day.

Elmo interacted with his team from time to time, but he felt it was never about the specifics of the AI project. Instead, the scientists came out as individuals, pairs, or small packs anytime they needed encouragement or a slight course adjustment.

One day a scientist beamed, "Dr. Michaelson, guess what? You won't believe it, but we have a blueprint for the robot dog puppies."

Another day, a scientist needed a simple nod from Elmo before they continued. "Um, sir, the chemical process for foraging and nutrient synthesis is complete and we have one option for a delivery system. What do you think?"

Elmo sat in the dirt, looked up and enjoyed each moment with his scientists. Every exchange ended with the scientist returning to the lab with an increased desire to explore their curiosities.

Occasionally, Elmo thought the scientists tried a bit too hard to impress or entertain him with their stories. Still, he never felt they embellished their accomplishments. In fact, he noticed they developed senses of humor tailored to make him laugh. He dismissed it as a silly thought and decided it must be a natural development of working together for so long. Finishing each other's sentences. Knowing how to hit a punch line and time it out to get a rise out of your longtime friend. That kind of thing.

Twenty-eight days after the launch of the AI robot dog project, the entire team entered the garden together. They stood in a semicircle, faces full of pride, and told Elmo they were ready to present the first beta test of the AI.

23

It was a different day. Time had flown since Elmo's team started working on the AI project and now it was time for a status update.

Elmo entered the conference room first thing in the morning and took his usual spot at the round table. It was the first time he didn't wear a lab coat in that room. Instead, he wore a button-down shirt and his signature straw hat. The change made him feel above the process, looking down on it, and more comfortably in charge.

His team of scientists sat on the edge of their seats, except Elmo, who lounged back in his chair. The team members shared looks of nervous tension. Elmo, by contrast, his face was lit with wonder, as though he was seeing a fancy science thing for the first time and was just happy to be along for the ride.

Rotund Dr. Cheong, the lead AI programmer, stood in front of the group to present the test. Rotund Dr. Cheong, who looked like an Asian scientist version of John Belushi, explained the concept of the test.

"Simple really. We have a closed system that contains only our AI entity and a sample human resources directory containing names and birthdates."

He continued, "We're going to ask the AI to find a name that's not in the directory. Then we'll record the AI's emotional response to frustration."

The room grew quiet and everyone leaned forward in their seat to catch every word from the speaker in the center of the table.

Rotund Dr. Cheong cleared his throat and began, "Mr. Carey? Hello, Mr. Carey?"

A voice came from the speaker, "Dr. Cheong, yes. I'm here."

Rotund Dr. Cheong replied, "Mr. Carey. I have a task for you. Would you please find a name in a database for me?"

The AI responded cheerfully, "Alllll-righty then. What's the name?"

Rotund Dr. Cheong smirked and said, "Last name, Huginkiss. First name, Amanda."

The room held its breath, the tension thick enough to taste like Snickers, if tension had a flavor.

After a few beats, the AI replied, "Sorry, Dr. Cheong, but I can't seem to find Amanda Huginkiss."

Rotund Dr. Cheong deadpanned, "Perhaps you should lower your standards."

A few scientists almost spoiled the fun when they couldn't hold back their chuckles.

From the speaker came a pause, then, "Wait a

minute. I'm looking for Amanda Huginkiss? A man… To hug… And kiss…"

The scientists erupted with a fit of knee-slapping laughter. Elmo mixed roars, wheezes, and snorts with his overwhelming enjoyment of the moment. Rotund Dr. Cheong stood an inch taller and adjusted his tie with a champion's smirk, ready to lead them to the next punchline. Their camaraderie, their humor—those were things that didn't exist in North Korean scientific environments until Elmo had formed his misfit team. They'd become a regular set of chuckleheads.

In the background of the scientists' laughter, Mr. Carey, the AI, really caught on. Through the speaker, he laughed along. "Dr. Cheong! You ass! That's brilliant! I'm not even mad. You totally got me!" Then Mr. Carey's voice shifted to a serious tone that cut through the laughter in the room, "Oh actually… No! I *am* mad! NO ONE PUNKS ME!"

Mr. Carey took control of the facility's utilities and intranet. The lights flickered, maniacal laughter blared from speakers throughout the building, and the monitors displayed horrifying, bloody imagery. Elmo and the scientists froze, and wore their most intense *oh shit* expressions.

Then, just as suddenly, the chaos ceased. The monitors switched to serene scenes of a spring meadow with butterflies and rainbows. Mr. Carey's voice returned, cheerful. "Ha-ha! Gotcha! You should see the looks on your faces! Snap!"

The humans at the table got even deeper looks of worry on their faces. Mr. Carey chuckled in the background.

Elmo mouthed to Rotund Dr. Cheong, "I thought you said it was a closed system?"

Rotund Dr. Cheong returned a squeamish smile and sheepish shrug to Elmo.

Mr. Carey kept on in the background, "Jeez, can't you guys take a joke? Anyway, totally sorry about that." Then under his breath, "Guess it's on me. Gotta know your audience." Then louder, "Hey, you guys, totally sorry."

Rotund Dr. Cheong straightened his tie one more time for effect and then asked Mr. Carey to "shut down for the day."

Mr. Carey hesitantly said, "Sure. But again. You know, totally sorry. Right? Everything cool between us?"

Rotund Dr. Cheong smiled and responded, "Mr. Carey, yeah, ice-cold cool."

Elmo, blown back in his chair, let out a big exhale, scratched his beard, then addressed the team, "Guess we got some bugs to work out. But a good start. I got two questions for you, Rotund Dr. Cheong. First, how much of that was scripted?"

Rotund Dr. Cheong grinned. "Only my opening round, trying to reel him in with the 'a man to hug and kiss' bit. Everything else, impromptu. Genuine interaction."

Elmo nodded. "Well, before the next question. Good job pulling that one off. That's a classic."

Rotund Dr. Cheong gave a small bow.

Elmo continued, "Second question. We were running this beta test in an isolated environment, right? And Mr. Carey still broke into the facility's utilities? So how do we know he shut himself down and isn't hiding in the network? We obviously can't control this AI."

Rotund Dr. Cheong answered, "Good question. If he didn't want to shut down, we'd have to turn off all the power to all the systems to shut him down. There's no way to find him if he doesn't want to be found."

Elmo said, "I have to be honest. I already love it. But do you think I should trust it?"

Rotund Dr. Cheong launched into an explanation of the AI's design and likened its trust and loyalty to the bond formed between a mother and child at birth. A moment of supreme trauma turned into comfort. He explained how they adapted the principle to the AI to ensure its loyalty by associating its master with relief from overwhelming sensory overload.

Rotund Dr. Cheong nodded to the rest of Elmo's team and said, "Maybe we left some holes in our explanation, but you already know the science, so let's skip ahead into how our AI robot dogs work.

"To make our AI trustworthy, each individual robot dog has a human master it will love so much, be so loyal to, it would die for that master. We do this by making the first memory in the robot dog's computer an experience of supreme sensory overload that takes them to the brink of a complete melt-down, then we avert the melt-down at the very moment they feel the biorhythms of their master. At that moment, supreme trauma turns into supreme comfort and their computer recognizes their master as the ultimate remedy to trauma.

"This makes the robot dogs the most loyal dogs in the world, or maybe as loyal as a well-trained biological dog. That's a subject our team has debated quite hotly for the last few weeks. Just how loyal can a biological dog be? And how would we objectively measure loyalty? But I digress. We all agree that there doesn't seem to be an answer we can reach using the scientific method because the robot dogs are light years ahead of biological dogs in nearly every way. Intelligence. Speed. Quickness—"

Elmo interrupted, "Wait a second. It sounds like you already have the robot dogs done. Like you already have a robot puppy prototype ready to be tested?"

Young Dr. Jung jumped in and stammered excitedly. "Not puppy. Maybe? We think? Yes. Not prototype. A lot. Whole robot puppy litter, finish? Yes. A lot. Ready for operation? Yes. A lot. Wait for your approval? Upload AI to robot puppy and operationalize? Yes. A lot. Trust and love? Yes, and yes. Maybe, we think, yes, a lot."

Elmo smiled ear to ear and said, "Damn, you guys are fucking awesome."

Rotund Dr. Cheong added, "That was just one of the AI personalities we built; the funny one. We've got the sickly one, sleepy, grumpy, the stupid one, the smart one, and bashful. Seven in all."

Elmo laughed. "You guys never stop amazing me! Bring 'em out! What are you waiting for?"

The rotund scientist replied, "We wanted to surprise you. If you approved of the AI beta test. You know, if it matched your vision, AI that you can love and trust, then we were going to ask for a day to upload the AI personalities and give you a full-on operations test."

Elmo said, "Perfect. What were you thinking, tomorrow morning? Anyway, yeah, I approve. You know where you can find me. Just get me from the garden. I can't wait. This is going to be awesome."

He looked around the room and marveled at how far the team had come. They were the first North Korean scientists to operate without centralized control since well before 1950. They proved they'd learned how to thrive as individuals on a team.

Elmo knocked his fist on the table twice and said, "I'm so proud of our team. So proud."

He got up and went back outside to give them the space they needed to get things done without his interference. Plus, his head buzzed with too much chaotic energy and he did not want to let his ungrounded mind accidentally muddy up his team's ability to concentrate during these crucial last steps.

24

With the afternoon sun baking down, Elmo sat on the ground in his garden and let dirt pour through his hands. He shifted it from his right to his left, then let it fall back to the earth. His mind was distracted, detached from the present moment.

The soil near the lab was sandy, its pH so acidic only scraggly patches of crabgrass and dandelions could survive. That was a trait of nearly all the soil throughout North Korea—a remnant of the country's self-reliant push to grow all its own food that depleted the land of nutrients. It made the topsoil of North Korea very much like the dirt in Iraq, which had never recovered from the Akkadian Empire's poor soil management.

This year the weather was particularly dry in East Asia. Even the monsoon season had only a few days of light rain. The ground, though sandy, was hard as cement, much like the arid terrain of Mosul.

Elmo stood up and brushed the dirt off of his pants. He got back to work, but he got his pickaxe stuck in the ground with the first swing so he sat back down in the dirt and let his mind wander.

Once he got his team up inside and his garden going outside, Elmo had spent his days working the garden by hand. He could've used machinery, but he preferred the physical labor. He dug with his shovel, and sometimes wielded a pickaxe to break the stubborn ground, and ended each day with a bone-deep exhaustion he hadn't felt since his deployments to the Middle East as a young man—those foolish days when he'd spent downtime breaking himself off, trying to join the Roger Bannister sub-four-minute mile club.

After meeting Sora, Elmo had slept very lightly, with powerful dreams that jolted him awake several times throughout the night. His mind used his dream space to help him digest the unpleasant certainty that North Korean authorities would someday torture him and Sora to death. In particular, Elmo did his best to deal with the possibility that the secret police could come in the night and end their lives at any time.

That was the same feeling, a complete lack of control over life and death, that kept him in a very light sleep all those nights, all those years ago, during deployments. The mortars rained down and randomly brought the reaper out for some unlucky bastard. It didn't help to ease the tension trying to fixate on the very small odds of getting hit. Listening to his heart made him even more anxious because his heart always emphasized how important it was for him to maintain constant vigilance until the mission completed.

Elmo's excitement during the AI beta test presentation had been genuine, but forced. It felt like a lifetime since he truly cared about AI, EMPs, or physics. Those pursuits no longer brought him happiness.

It reminded him of his mid-career military intelligence work—when he realized the thrill of completing a classified mission was hollow. All the secret stuff only provided a masturbation type of high. A one-night stand type of happiness. A dopamine fueled manic pursuit, followed by a rush of adrenaline, but nearly completely absent of oxytocin comfort and serotonin contentment. Elmo didn't like that high anymore. In fact, he despised it.

Grateful though he was for his team, he knew their bond was temporary. Like a deployment, their shared mission would end. They'd go their separate ways, and there'd be no way to rekindle what they had. Just like what he had with his teams of collectors and analysts during his military days. People he had to let go of, names and faces he could barely remember. Seeing the inevitable loss on the horizon was an extra weight on Elmo's mind.

Elmo sat in the dirt of his garden. He wished he could hit fast forward, have all the bull-crap subtracted from his life, and be in a safe place eating a nice, hot meal with his Sora. He said "to hell with it" and used his bare hands to get the pickaxe unstuck from the ground. Elmo swept and rubbed away thin layers of sand. His index finger rested on a groove in the pick-axe's steel, and he froze, lost in thought.

The groove reminded him of the trigger on his M4 rifle and brought his scattered thoughts into sharp focus. His mind aligned with truths he'd avoided for years: that life offered no guarantees, and the only way to increase the odds of future happiness was to make the right decisions in the present.

Elmo had arrived at this moment through a funky combination of physics, chemistry, fate, and free will. And he had to accept that, no matter how hard he worked, or how well he planned, he lived in a world that didn't make promises for the future.

Logically, Elmo understood that. Emotionally, it was harder. The desire for control—especially in life-and-death circumstances—was nearly impossible to quiet. His mind raced, analyzed every thought and action, tried to eliminate uncertainty and ensure survival. The task grew so immense his brain threatened to collapse under the weight of it until it instinctively shifted to an algorithm of deeper reflection.

For the rest of the day, Elmo stared into space, ran through the chain of events that had shaped his life. He began with childhood truths: DNA, family, a small Midwestern town. His late birthday made him a late bloomer, too old to compete for local sports glory. Academics didn't impress girls in his town, so he drifted toward drugs instead. That path led him to the Army to escape a loser's life of weed, cocaine, and crack.

Then it was the Army's truths that shaped his twenties and thirties and shut down so much of his creativity. Then it was the depression he'd tried to drink his way through once he realized the Army was just a stupid rank game that served a nation that had become economically reliant on the military-industrial complex to stay on top in the world. Soldiers were pawns in war games that might leave them dead in the desert of some shit hole country, where they risked their lives forcing some foreign peoples to accept a social system that didn't match their respective cultural values. And the headache inducing mental gymnastics he did to ignore the truth that the wars in the Middle East were all about keeping oil prices tied to the US dollar, not about democracy.

Then it was the decision to double down, dig deeper and deeper into the realms of the classified clandestine world, go top-secret sub-gama behind the curtain to meet the wizard of oz and chase the white rabbit into every real conspiracy you could imagine.

Then it was that marriage to that older woman. Fifteen years into that marriage, he found out he and that woman weren't truly in love, but merely tried to create a shared lie and run away from their respective pasts. Then her physically and emotionally abusing him whenever he inadvertently uncovered a new truth about her past. Then he used distance and numbing techniques whenever she discovered unpleasant truths about him.

Then the divorce. And then the deeper depression. It felt like he amounted to nothing as a kid or an adult. Elmo found he'd wasted all his best years building meaningless sandcastles. Then he chose a boozed-out isolation where the voices found him. Then the excessive prayer that made the voices worse and brought more demons. It was like his prayers yelled out on the spiritual battlefield, "Hey motherfuckers, Elmo is here, and he stands for God, Jesus, and the Holy Spirit! If you got a problem with that, then bring your best." Oh, and the demons, they sure as fuck brought the fucking pain. Then he lived in the van where, thank the Creator of all, the Master and forgiving Force, because He made the voices become one voice. A perfectly accepted blend of Elmo's light and dark. The voice led him to go back to college. Get into physics. Go to North Korea. Meet Sora, the love of this life.

Elmo sat in his garden, aware that people somewhere likely plotted against him. He had no control over their intentions. The best he could do was breathe through the uncertainty, keep his body busy, and look forward to holding Sora in their bed at the end of the day. He was thankful for her love, even when he knew it might not last forever.

Elmo's stare broke when Sora pulled him out of his algorithm with a tap him on the shoulder. Elmo looked up at his Sora, and tears streamed down his cheeks.

Sora didn't need an explanation. Without a word, she sat down in the dirt next to him. The dogs got really close to Elmo and boobied up against him. Barklee, that silly mutt, did a pass by and let his tail hit Elmo in the face a few times before he licked Elmo's cheeks with a slobber packed apology kiss and nudged in close to get the best boobied position, his head in Elmo's lap.

Elmo looked at the dogs. Then at Sora. He reached his dirty, gritty, calloused hands over and took up Sora's hand in his. Elmo scooted, and the dogs scooted over with him until he was side by side and up against Sora. She activated her own thousand-mile stare. Sora was still writing her own algorithm, laying out the cause-and-effect relationships and series of intersecting vectors that brought her together with Elmo.

Tears fell silently from both their eyes, though neither sobbed. Elmo's mind captioned the memory as the happiest moment of his life, even as he accepted that their story might not have a happy ending.

For hours, they sat together in quiet communion before they finally got up to walk home. Their silence was heavy but peaceful. Someday, they'd figure it all out—a shared algorithm to understand how they'd come together.

25

When Elmo and Sora got home, they left the lights off and showered together in the dark.

They didn't leave an inch untouched on each other's bodies. Every itch scratched. Every surface scrubbed. They used hard pressure on the smelliest, least delicate areas: the feet and armpits. And light soapy fingertip circles over each other's more sensitive places. At moments, their breathing synchronized, quickened into soft, rapid pants before it settled back into steady, calm rhythms. Elmo didn't attempt to wash Sora's long, flowing jet-black hair—he knew his limits. Washing a woman's hair in the shower was outside his expertise, and he didn't want to ruin the moment.

After stepping out of the shower, they patted each other off with towels. Sora took her time with the hair dryer. Elmo was happy to wait for his turn to use the dryer on his beard because he loved how Sora always gave so much attention to getting all the knots out of her hair. Maybe his favorite thing in the world was running his fingers through her silky, knot-free strands, marveling at how effortlessly they flowed. He appreciated the effort she put into her beauty, always impressed by her attention to detail.

He hoped he would grow old with her. Elmo knew the years would make him an old man long before Sora's vibrant youth faded. He hoped she'd forgive him for that.

After he draped on his bathrobe, Elmo handed Sora the plastic applicator stick from the home pregnancy kit that Old Dr. Jeong had procured for them. The whole team of scientists knew Elmo and Sora got the test kit. The entire team knew baby news may or may not come soon. In North Korea, people kept meticulous secrets from the authorities, but among trusted friends, nothing stayed hidden. Even the scientists, brilliant and disciplined, shared the need for community and mutual understanding.

Sora sat on the toilet, leaned to the side, released the pressure valve on her bladder, and held the plastic applicator in her urine stream. When she finished, she handed the plastic applicator to Elmo and finished her tinkle.

Elmo held the dripping wet stick out so they could watch the results together in the faint moonlight spilling into the bathroom.

Slowly, a blue line appeared.

Sora was pregnant.

Elmo stood barefoot on the cold tile and his mind

swam. *I hope it's a boy. But hell, a girl, that would be scary as hell, but yeah, a girl too. Either way, we're gonna have a hell-raiser. A cool-handed little guy or gal. Born to do some world-shaking.*

Sora sprayed her booty clean with the bidet and then pat dried it with a tissue. She sat on the toilet in silent contemplation, thinking about the reaction she wanted to show to Elmo. Then she realized she was already reacting. Her smile was so big, her face muscles pulled so hard and stretched her lips ear to ear, that it hurt her cheeks, but she couldn't find a conscious control mechanism in her brain to stop the happiness from completely conquering her. She thought, *I hope Elmo likes the name Lukas for a boy and maybe Jisu for a girl.*

That night, Elmo fell asleep with his head resting on Sora's belly, her fingers gently stroking his hair. They were so caught up in the moment, so consumed by the enormity of their shared happiness, that they didn't give a single thought to the surveillance equipment hidden in their home—or the analysts endlessly combing through their private lives.

26

Kɪᴍ Yᴇᴏ Jᴇᴏɴɢ sat in her private office and her eye twitched uncontrollably as she watched a direct feed of the surveillance tape from Elmo's house.

A few days prior, she had replaced the intelligence analysts stationed under Elmo's house with her own handpicked showbiz team. North Korea's security and intelligence resources were stretched thin, and most of their focus directed at the insurance of her brother's safe navigation of the summit meetings and to analyze the unprecedented global attention the country received. When she stepped in with her trusted people, Kim Yeo Jeong not only earned favors from overwhelmed officials, but ensured herself full control over Elmo and Sora's surveillance.

It wasn't the surveillance mission that stressed her—it was the storm that brewed inside her.

Her eye twitched because of all the brainpower she forcefully directed toward the developments between Elmo and Sora and away from her deeply seated hatred that rapidly grew at how badly her brother regularly victimized her.

Her legal pad laid open on the desk in front of her, filled with lines and patterns that mirrored her erratic thoughts: slow, methodical strokes alternated with fast, frantic vectors and inward spirals. If her tangled emotions had formed into words, they might have sounded something like this:

I won't let this slip. I'm never losing again—not to anyone. No more golden showers. No more praying for forgiveness. This is my show now. Fuck my brother. Fuck the Party. I'm going to win.

With the pregnancy test footage, Kim Yeo Jeong had the most genuine moment of happiness ever captured on tape in her possession. They'd wired the house for total surveillance, giving her not just a single clip but a wealth of data: close-ups, heat maps, sensitive audio, and a library of historical context. She and her team meticulously processed every detail of Elmo and Sora's lives and analyzed the shifts in their rhythm after the pregnancy discovery.

It wasn't just a piece of television—it was revolutionary. No audience had ever received such an intimate window into real, unscripted human joy. As Sora's agent, Kim Yeo Jeong had complete authority over how they would present the footage. In her mind, it was the key to launch North Korea as the world's capital for genuine artistic expression.

Netflix was essential to the plan. She had a direct

line to their top executives, who no longer dared to call her after too many unanswered attempts. On the other hand, they could not afford to ignore her calls. She also knew they couldn't afford her next demands—but they couldn't afford to lose Sora either.

At 2:00 a.m. North Korea time, Kim Yeo Jeong initiated a conference call with Netflix's top brass. She let the silence linger for a beat before she began, with her tone icy and command voice: "This is Kim Yeo Jeong. I have in my possession the most important piece of entertainment in the history of mankind. Before I share a sample, here are my demands."

Kim Yeo Jeong let the Netflix executives wait in silence for a beat again while she gathered the air to rattled off an uninterrupted list of her conditions. "First, you will establish a sister company headquartered in North Korea. Your operation will be *Netflix West*. We will be *Netflix East*. I will be the CEO of Netflix East, but you'll provide me with a team of your best consultants to help me establish the initial operations. I will use them for as long as I see necessary, then I'll choose who will stay on my team and who should return to your Netflix West operations. Second, you'll invest in our people. Give our nation a high-speed internet capability that provides every one of our citizens the ability to stream our content. Top to bottom. The whole package. Warehouses with servers and carbon-neutral cooling systems. Hardwire delivery to every home in my country. Wireless delivery to every corner of my country, 5G towers. Tablets. Smartphones. Desktops. Smart TVs. All our citizens will receive free access to Netflix East so they can stay connected with our stars."

The Netflix executives shook their heads in silent objection to the outrageous demands. All the Netflix people had stopped taking notes when Kim Yeo Jeong proposed Netflix East. They knew Kim Yeo Jeong's production of Sora's content was a golden goose, but it was too audacious for them to accept.

Kim Yeo Jeong remained calm. She would get everything she wanted. She knew they would beg at her feet once they saw her content presentation because she knew very intimately how far people would go to get their next fix once a product hooked them and, at that point, everyone in the world, including the Netflix executives, were addicted to Sora.

Not only did everyone have their favorite show starring Sora, but they also had a favorite commentary show that discussed some aspect of her life. Wives, moms, sisters, and daughters wore Sora's fashion. Even if you didn't own a dog, you still signed up for the newsletters that highlighted the latest dog food and pooch products Sora recommended.

The Netflix people believed they could maintain their composure if the possibility of losing access to Sora developments came into play. In their daily briefs and strategy sessions, the Netflix officials had prepped for the good possibility that Kim Yeo Jeong would make some outlandish demands. They also had several contingency plans for the high likelihood Sora would get pregnant someday. Everyone already dealt with this potential plot twist in Sora's life because it was such a hot topic on most talk shows. Names. Boy or Girl. Twins. Oh, I hope it's twins. Why just twins? Why not triplets? Anyway. Even ESPN's top sportscasters had diverted their careers to give us live commentary on Sora's life.

In this teleconference call, Kim Yeo Jeong asked, "Are you ready?" And she hit play.

Her trailer filled the screen in the Netflix boardroom. The video was a masterpiece: a montage of Elmo and Sora's love story, tastefully rendered with CGI effects that built suspense as it culminated in the pregnancy test. The final shot lingered on the couple's eyes, and left the outcome ambiguous. Was it joy? Fear? Disappointment? The audience could interpret it however they wanted.

The presentation did not tell the audience whether the couple was pregnant.

Kim Yeo Jeong ended the call after one statement: "You won't receive another second of footage until you meet my demands."

She knew the trailer alone would feed the hype. Even if Netflix leaked it, it would only strengthen her position. And when the executives frantically tried to call her back, she let the phone ring. She wanted them to sweat.

She sat back and wondered how she'd tell her brother about all these developments. She wished she wouldn't have to tell him. Hoped something, anything, a real miracle of sorts would come to her so she wouldn't have to pray for the Great Leader's blessings ever again.

She made a few more vector scribbles on the notepad before her hand froze in place and her eye twitch ceased. A childhood memory surfaced and filled her mind: the most important lesson her father taught her. The times she was on his lap playing with her authentic USA barbies.

The quiet precious moments Kim Jong Il lovingly stroked his little Yeo Jeong's hair. His princess. Daddy's special girl. He told her, "You're my best. I wish you had been born a son. What a Great Leader you would have become. You have the mind. You were born with the instinct, the same your grandfather had. Maybe it skips a generation. It's a recessive gene in my DNA. But you have it. You know how to win an audience. How to hold their attention with the good. That's the best way to get power, to hold it eternally. Win the hearts of the people with genuine warmth. Boy, I wish you were born a boy. Your stupid brother. Father, bless him, he thinks it's all pain and pleasure. Doesn't understand nuance. Guess he gets that from me. Ha! But you, my princess, my gem, you're my reminder of the true greatness of our bloodline. You have your grandfather's sense of charm. While not trying to please, while staying true, while staying strong. But also, my strength, my raw, ugly understanding of the true nature of this world."

"Daddy, you give me too much. Your wisdom is what saves."

"Haha, my Yeo Jeong, so perfect with words. Haha. How do you like your barbies, my princess?"

"Daddy, I made a play with the barbies. It's called, 'Daddy's girl.' But you are the star. But it is not complete unless there's an Asian man doll, an Asian Ken doll. Handsome like you. With that doll, I can show the play."

"Haha, no, my daughter, they don't make an Asian Ken doll."

"Then… I will make one! You are the love of the play. The center of my story."

"Haha. You even play me, my princess?"

"No!" she cried. "No, daddy. I do not lie to you. And I do not manipulate you. I hide the truth from the audience, because they're not ready until the story makes them ready. Then truth makes the ending real. The raw ugliness makes the story beautiful. But it saves for the end. Except with you. I give you truth from the beginning."

"Oh, my Yeo Jeong, what a Great Leader you would've made. Hahaha. Too bad for your vagina. If only it had been a penis. Such a world-changing difference that dangling piece of flesh makes. Haha."

The memory gave her resolve. No one outside her

team needed to know about the pregnancy. Preventing leaks would be easy if she kept her crew locked down, isolated from their families and friends, and on tight shifts with no downtime.

Nothing her father taught her helped with the biggest decision: should she tell her brother before she finalized the deal?

She knew if she played it wrong, she'd end up just like her other family members who didn't follow proper protocol. Like her uncle, Jang Sung Thaek or her half-brother, Kim Jong-nam. It would be a very professional death. Just a matter of politics. A legal matter. Nothing personal.

Not even a world class team of statisticians could help Kim Yeo Jeong calculate the potential risks and rewards for doing her business in North Korea. Not when success and failure were measured in terms of life and death, not dollars and cents. Not when, in North Korea, sometimes making money could get you in more trouble than losing money.

Kim Yeo Jeong tightened her ponytail and grit her teeth as cold clarity settled in. She thought, *is this a billion dollar deal? No, try a trillion.*

Kim Yeo Jeong decided to set up a morning house call with Elmo and Sora. She needed to gauge whether her stars were prepared for the rough road ahead—or if it was safer to abandon the opportunity entirely.

27

Sora and Elmo woke up in each other's arms minutes before the alarm clock went off. It was the best sleep they had since their first night together.

Elmo stepped out of bed, scratched and stretched, and almost stomped on Barklee, who always fell asleep right in the place you would plant your foot. Elmo went into the bathroom to empty his bladder.

Sora left the bedroom with her dogs at her side. A chef on his knees in the living room arranged a tray of freshly cut fruit on the coffee table and greeted them with a smile. And next to the chef, Kim Yeo Jeong sat on the couch with a cup of tea.

The smell of citrus tipped the dogs off to their presence, and Daisuki made sure the visitors did not surprise Sora. Daisuki flashed a quick warning grin at the uninvited guests before she looked up and at Sora to communicate a few soft barks. Sora responded to Daisuki, "I know, girl. Kim Yeo Jeong knows. And it'll be okay."

Sora sat in the chair next to the couch. Kim Yeo

Jeong slid a hot cup of coffee toward Sora, and Sora took it up and slowly sipped it.

Kim Yeo Jeong called out toward the bathroom, "Good morning, Elmo. Please come out to the living room so we can discuss Sora's pregnancy."

Hearing Kim Yeo Jeong's call startled Elmo so much that he fumbled his wiener and got pee all over the front of his pajama bottoms.

Elmo washed up hastily and came out to the living room in a new pair of pants to stand behind Sora and the dogs. He crossed his arms and had the mindset of a Texas hold 'em player who hoped he would get some cards to complement his hand.

Kim Yeo Jeong looked at the couple and got straight to the point. "I know Sora is pregnant. Her pregnancy, your relationship, the dogs, all of it. This is a gold mine. No, this is alchemy. I'd like to be honest with you. But first, you need to be honest with me. Elmo, what do you expect to work on after you produce AI robot dogs for the Party?"

"I don't have anything else to work on, only my garden and its soil."

"What do you expect to happen to you and Sora once you complete this AI project and don't have any new things to offer the Party?"

"I expect your brother to have Sora and I killed unless someone convinces him he still needs us."

Kim Yeo Jeong responded with a scornful *tsk* and

a slow shake of her head. It never ceased to displease her when Elmo was a source of disrespectful honesty.

Daisuki and Barklee boobied up next to Sora, and the three shared half purring, half growling noises that allowed them to reassure each other that things would be fine.

Kim Yeo Jeong continued, "I do not know of any plans to have you killed. Why should I believe you know more about my brother's intentions than me?"

Elmo looked around the room and nodded at the places where surveillance cameras were obviously located. Elmo continued, "You know everything about me. I have nothing to hide. I passed all your background checks. Passed your polygraph tests. You know, for a short period it was my job to study the Kim family, which included a focus on your brother's time at Swiss boarding school. Still, I only had simple knowledge about his eating habits and grades, nothing significant to report. But after personally serving under his command all this time, I can tell you I know his utmost intention is to lead the Korean people to greatness. At any cost, he'll make sure he crushes his enemies in such a way that he and the Party are loved and respected as a righteous, great fatherly force. Am I missing anything?"

Kim Yeo Jeong responded, "Yes, and we know everything about you. And I say with confidence, you hold true to your profile. You still haven't learned your lesson. After all this time, you have no fear of authority or fear of facing the consequences of your actions. You still believe some supernatural power will charge your imagination and save you from your stupidity."

Elmo smiled at Sora and the dogs and then responded to Kim Yeo Jeong, "My brain is certainly arrogant. Luckily, I listen to my heart now." Elmo laughed too hard, out of place, and slapped his knee.

Kim Yeo Jeong said, "There's nothing to laugh at. I came here to discuss serious business."

Elmo interrupted her, "Of course you did. Kim Yeo Jeong, always serious. Never letting herself put together the big picture puzzle. Never allowing her heart to express its love for stories with happy endings." Elmo stopped his laughter and sat down in front of the couch next to the dogs at Sora's feet.

Kim Yeo Jeong said, "Now I see it was all in vain. I cannot trust you. I am so sorry for you, Sora, for having fallen for this crazy man who only leaves unfulfilled potential and disastrous ruin in his path."

Kim Yeo Jeong stood and brushed the dust off her pants suit. She took one curt step toward the door, but stopped when Sora yelled, "Wait! Barklee wants to tell you something before you go!"

Kim Yeo Jeong turned slowly and displayed all her disappointment in her stare.

Sora continued, "Barklee says, he says, he wants everyone to know, you can kill a dog if you feed it chocolate."

Kim Yeo Jeong scoffed at Sora. "What's that

supposed to mean? Don't tell me Elmo is rubbing off on you, and you've lost your mind too. Saying the most ridiculous things out of context all the time. Listen, Elmo, Sora, your pregnancy gives us a show that is essentially a license to print money."

A dazed look of wonder came over Elmo's face. It all made sense. He gave Barklee a deep, thankful scratch behind the ears, then addressed Kim Yeo Jeong, "I am sorry. You obviously came here to help us reach a new deal. Something big."

Elmo stopped and reached up to take Sora's hand in his. She nodded at him. Elmo continued, "Please arrange the deal with Netflix. We won't let you down. As a measure of good faith, you can see the AI robot dog test this morning, and I'm sure it will impress you. Then I will present the AI robot dogs to your brother. I am confident I'll have another trick up my sleeve that convinces your brother to keep us alive. Please tell him these *exact* words. With my help, the true leader of the Communist Party will make Korea's greatest enemies eat shit and die."

Kim Yeo Jeong repeated the words with a snort of a laugh. "With your help, my brother can force Korea's greatest enemies to eat shit and die. That's what you want me to tell him?"

Elmo said, "Yes, and tell him to expect the AI robot presentation when he returns to Korea. Timing is important. The enemies of the Korean people are always scheming. We can't afford to stop the pace of progress while we have victory so close at hand."

Kim Yeo Jeong said, "Now you almost sound North Korean! Ha! Okay, I'll tell him. And yes, we'll move forward with Netflix. Sora, as your agent, with your consent, I'll make your pregnancy and motherhood into a show worthy of the genuine content you have provided me."

Sora responded with a, "Yup, yup, yup!" and a laugh. Her Barklee was such a clown. He reminded her so much of that little pooch Franklin who saved her from forced prostitution. Sora laughed and repeated under her breath, "You can kill a dog if you feed it chocolate." Sora wondered how Elmo understood the clue. She wondered if he also knew how to communicate with the dogs. Sora decided she'd ask him to explain sometime when they finally got a break from all the action that seemed to pack every minute of their lives together.

28

Elmo took Sora's hand and gave her some gentlemanly help down the front porch steps. She had never liked this type of gesture before, but with the new baby in her belly, for some reason, it felt appropriate to have a chivalrous man.

Elmo glanced at his wristwatch. It was 04:50. Even if they walked fast, he'd be late for work for the first time in his life. The early summer air was chilly, so Sora wore her new favorite cardigan sweater over her sundress.

There were no makeup sessions, costumes, or filming scheduled for Sora and her dogs. They had classified the AI robot beta test as a matter of national security and there was no room for errors, so Kim Yeo Jeong put her film crew on house arrest to keep them away from the lab and its grounds.

Sora glanced down at her doggies and smiled. Daisuki returned the smile, but Barklee's tail wagged furiously as he spoke in his excitable dog way: "One good throw? Please? Just one, then I won't ask again.

I'll be a good boy. One good fetcher! I've been such a good boy! Huh? Huh? How about it?"

"No, boy," Sora scolded lightly. "We're already running late."

Elmo kneeled on one knee and scratched Barklee behind the ear. He spoke to Sora but looked at the mutt. "I don't know. One good toss ain't gonna hurt anybody."

Barklee didn't wait for a reversal. He ran off and barked out happily, "Oh boy. Oh boy. A fetcher. Oh boy, oh boy." He grabbed the biggest stick he could find in the front yard and ran back toward Elmo at a full tilt, stick in his mouth, slobbering, and panting with a huge happy dog smile.

Without breaking stride, Barklee dropped the stick two feet in front of Elmo, then leaped in the air to become "rocket dog," and score a direct hit, with his snout hammer punching Elmo's groin.

Elmo keeled over, grabbed his balls with both hands, winced in pain, and yelled, "Barklee! You asshole!"

Sora rubbed Elmo's back with her developing motherly touch, and half-laughed, half-scolded the dog. Barklee, however, couldn't help himself. He knew the rocket dog groin smash always brought out Elmo's best fetch throws.

Once Elmo finished coughing and most of the stinging pain left his balls, he picked up the stick and channeled all his anger into his throwing arm. Barklee and Daisuki sat obediently, both with their mouths closed and their eyes locked onto the stick.

Elmo pump faked a throw to the right, but neither dog flinched. It was obvious Elmo needed to bring his A+ game. He spun like a shot-putter and charged forward like a javelin thrower, then launched the stick in a direction the dogs didn't expect.

Daisuki caught the direction first, but Barklee quickly copied her correct calculus and broke out in a sprint that left the preggers Daisuki to trot in his dust. However, Barklee slowed his approach when he was halfway to the stick and pretended to be out of breath. Daisuki trotted past Barklee and got a step on the mutt, and he let her stay a beat ahead, so she was the first to get her mouth on that delicious stick. However, before Daisuki could run back with the prize, Barklee took two hard charging steps, bit part of the stick, and started some light tug-of-war action with Daisuki.

After three or four tugs, Daisuki growled like only a pregnant, annoyed bitch could growl, and Barklee immediately gave her full possession of the stick. Daisuki trotted back toward Elmo and Sora and held the stick in her cheeky Shiba smile.

As they stood on the walkway, Sora leaned into Elmo. Elmo put one arm around Sora's waist, one hand on her belly, and circled his finger around one of the cool, smooth buttons on Sora's sweater. Sora and Elmo shared a smile and then looked out at their silly pups.

"What's that rascal Barklee doing?" Sora asked.

Barklee had chased down Daisuki and gently grabbed one end of the stick. Instead of pulling, he matched his pace to hers—an uneven mix of full, half, and quarter trots—so they could return the stick together. They dropped it at Elmo's feet in perfect unison.

Elmo didn't pay attention to them, though. He brushed his hand through Sora's silky hair and gave her a light kiss on her forehead.

Hand in hand, Elmo and Sora stepped over the stick and walked down the path. Daisuki stayed at their side as they walked toward the lab, but Barklee kept a good distance ahead so he could give himself some space to think. Barklee didn't want his family to know yet, but he gave serious consideration to retiring from the fetch game altogether. He'd get lost in the possibility of going out on top, leaving the game only after he achieved the unachievable, perfect fetch. He also wondered if he'd have the time required to maintain his standard of perfection after his puppies were born.

Daisuki silently worried too. She'd overheard Sora mention the AI robot dogs weeks ago. About how they designed them to be exact replicas of her future puppies. Daisuki hoped she wouldn't fail some motherly task and find out she wasn't fit to raise the real puppies in her belly.

Elmo tried to focus on the events of the day, but the possibility that he'd have to give something up to be a good dad distracted him. "*Luckily,*" he thought, "*it would be easy to step away from science if the AI robots were truly loveable and trustworthy.*"

Every few steps, Sora squeezed Elmo's hand and patted her belly with her free hand. She tried to remember where she saw the yoga routines recommended for expecting mothers. Sora believed if she maintained a healthy, vibrant lifestyle throughout the pregnancy, it would help ensure her baby wasn't born with a natural tendency for anxiety. She was determined to do everything within her power to make sure her baby entered the world with a calm, resilient mindset—one who could face the inevitable revelations about Mommy's past life.

•   •   •

Elmo, Sora, Barklee, and Daisuki all snapped out of their daze when they arrived at the lab and saw the AI robot dog presentation awaited them. They had arranged three lawn chairs and a set of portable bleachers on the front lawn. Seven scientists sat on the cold, uncomfortable aluminum bleachers and rocked back and forth. Kim Yeo Jeong occupied one of the lawn chairs, sat upright with impeccable posture, looked at her wristwatch, and waited to see if Elmo would run out of time.

Elmo and Sora took their seats in the lawn chairs beside Kim Yeo Jeong, who shook her head and let out a loud huffy breath to greet their unexcused tardiness.

Rotund Dr. Cheong stood in front of the crowd, looked off in the distance, silently mouthed his script, and practiced the hand gestures and choreography he planned to use for the presentation. Beside him, the AI robot puppies stood frozen in a military style formation. They looked like stuffed and mounted lifeless puppies, down to their blank, forward stares. They each had a unique coat design of fall colored fur in patterns that would make each dog the perfect fit for the name "patches" or maybe, "rusty."

Behind Rotund Dr. Cheong and the formation of robot puppies were three circus-style rings set up as test stations. In the first ring, a loaf of bread sat on a table and next to the table, a two-meter-tall section of triple-layered bulletproof glass. The middle ring showcased a five-ton military truck parked next to a fire hydrant prop. In the third ring, a Westminster dog show type obstacle course held runways, ramps, hoops, and hurdles.

Once everyone was seated and situated, Rotund Dr. Cheong retrieved a remote control from his pocket, gave a slight bow, and addressed the group with his best showman voice.

"Good morning, esteemed colleagues, Dr. Michaelson, Sora, and the great Kim Yeo Jeong. I give you AI robot dogs that—wait a second, Sora—could you please ask Barklee and Daisuki to remain calm and next to you for the duration of the show? Also, we designed special doggy earmuffs for them to wear.

The show will be loud so, could you please help us? For their safety."

Sora responded with a nod, and at her command, the two dogs laid down at her side. Sora realized the purpose of the headphones that hung on the armrest of her lawn chair. The dogs obediently let her set up their ear protection, which looked like old-school leather, football helmets adorned with space-aged LED lights evenly dispersed across its surface.

Rotund Dr. Cheong bowed again and continued, "I give you AI robot dogs you can *love—and trust!*" He pressed a button on the remote and triggered a burst of pyrotechnic rockets in front of the bleachers. The *BOOM*, flash, flares, and smoke made everyone cough, waft, and wipe tears away from their eyes.

From the smoke emerged the clumsy puppies that tripped, trotted, and yipped as they rushed the crowd. The whole litter of patchy puppies swarmed their target: Kim Yeo Jeong. The puppies jumped all over her and covered her with lickies and chewies. Instinct overwhelmed Kim Yeo Jeong, and her poker face came down for the first time in years.

The whole crowd of scientists broke into a chorus of ooos, coos, and awes while Kim Yeo Jeong tried to give all the perfect puppies a fair share of her affectionate pets. So many scruffy little ears. So many soul healing little tongues slobbered up her fingers and face. The flood of puppies knocked her over and out of her chair and she was all giggles and rolled around with them in the grass.

The excitement slowed to a manageable pace and Kim Yeo Jeong sat up with one puppy who refused to leave her lap. Kim Yeo Jeong looked into the little girl's eyes and it was clear; Kim Yeo Jeong had chosen the runt of the litter to be her puppy to love forever.

Rotund Dr. Cheong put two fingers in his mouth and chirped a show stopping whistle. All but one of the dogs fumbled, stumbled back to the front and center for the presentation. The runt took a nap in Kim Yeo Jeong's lap because "all the excitement musta tuckered the little girl out."

Rotund Dr. Cheong did a ring master's strut over to the lawn chairs and took a knee next to Kim Yeo Jeong and asked, "There's pure love in that dog's eyes, right?"

Kim Yeo Jeong responded, "I can't believe those are robots. There's no way those are robots. This better not be some kind of trick."

Rotund Dr. Cheong, who spoke with more familiarity than was customary when one addressed a member of the Kim family, asked, "It's the eyes? Isn't it?"

Kim Yeo Jeong, with a tone of angry disbelief, said, "Oh, I get it. Its some kind of computer trick? Manipulating me, right? I knew it."

Rotund Dr. Cheong stayed calm and said, "This presentation is all about dog tricks. But this puppy's love for you is authentic, not a trick."

The runt woke up from its quick nap, gave Kim Yeo Jeong a sloppy kiss on the cheek, and the robot puppy's chemically enhanced, oxytocin enriched slobber wiped away all of Kim Yeo Jeong's lingering doubts. The puppy wiggled out of her hands, plopped down to the ground and trip trotted to join her brothers and sisters up front in formation.

Kim Yeo Jeong got back up into her lawn chair and didn't bother to brush the grass off her pants suit or straighten her hair. For the rest of the presentation, she sat on the edge of her seat, elbows on her knees, and chin in her hands. She watched her puppy play with her brothers and sisters. Kim Yeo Jeong got lost in dreams about all the adventures she'd share with her new best friend.

Rotund Dr. Cheong started the presentation in the first ring to showcase the robot dogs' multifunction laser beam vision. He stood between the table and the wall of bulletproof glass and held a slice of bread up in the air. The biggest puppy in the litter jumped forward and red laser beams shot out of his eyes. The puppy's head oscillated so he could use his laser beam vision to toast the bread held in Rotund Dr. Cheong's outstretched hand evenly. Once the toast was golden brown, the puppy yipped and ran back to the formation and his tail wagged. Then the eyes on all the robot puppies glowed red. Beams of blazing light shot out of the puppy formation and with coordinated precision, the puppies' burned quick, sharp cuts through the wall of bulletproof glass.

Without missing a beat, the robot puppies followed Rotund Dr. Cheong into the second ring, where Kim Yeo Jeong's runt ran up to the military truck, yipped two little yips, and playfully bit a hole in the front tire. Rotund Dr. Cheong grabbed his belly and laughed like Santa Claus, while the other puppies broke from formation and teamed up to use their little jaws to rip the rest of the tire to shreds.

In the third ring, the puppies lined up, shed their puppy mannerisms, and went through the obstacle course. The puppies, one by one, with perfect presence and grace, ran down the ramp, jumped through the hoops, and over the hurdles. After they completed the course, each puppy crossed the finish line and blasted off into the air, up and out of sight. Small rocket pads on their paws allowed them to fly like Iron Man.

When the last one had blasted off, Rotund Dr. Cheong used his remote to cue the song "*The Final Countdown*" by Europe. Right as soon as the horns, drums, and guitars hit the first crescendo of the epic 80s rock hit, Rotund Dr. Cheong used the microphone function of his remote and said, "AI! Robot! Dogs!" The crowd stood up and hooted, and hollered. Then the puppies landed back on earth. Each stood tall and held a regal pose as more fireworks went off.

Elmo was on his feet and went hoarse with elated cheers. Sora got out of her seat and took a knee next to Barklee and Daisuki, who, despite the ear protection, still needed a hand to comfort and help them make it through the overwhelming sights and sounds.

Then, through the booms of fireworks, Daisuki, Barklee, and Sora heard the same little chorus voices, spoken in the silent telepathic dog language, *"Sorry. We just wanted to show off. Was it okay? How did we do, Mommy?"*

Daisuki responded in her instinctual motherly tone, *"You did great sweethearts. I'm so proud of you."*

Barklee, Daisuki, and Sora heard a chorus of happy yips from the robot puppies, who, with their mommy's acknowledgement, felt so accomplished.

The fireworks sputtered out and Rotund Dr. Cheong gave one slow bow. Sora took the headphones off Daisuki and Barklee. The two dogs ran forward to greet the robot puppies, who dropped their performance poses and ran to meet their mommy and daddy for the first time. Daisuki and Barklee swam around the puppy swarm and sniffed their butts in utter disbelief that they weren't real dogs. They did their best to hide any concern and confusion from the puppies. However, the sensory overload made Daisuki throw up. Barklee ran to his bitch's side and lapped up her puke. The robot puppies didn't understand why Mommy was sick.

Rotund Dr. Cheong powered down the robot dogs with a button on his remote. The lifelike creatures froze mid-step, their charm replaced by creepy stillness.

Sora gathered Barklee and Daisuki and tried to

soothe their shot nerves. She knew they needed to head inside the lab to get a break from the excitement and confusion of the morning. However, before she left, Sora addressed Elmo and his team. "This is truly amazing and terrifying. I don't know how you did it, but those are real dogs."

Elmo nodded. "Thank you, Sora." When she walked away, he turned to the scientists in the bleachers. He asked, "I can easily see how we can use these AI robots as guard dogs for elite Party members, but how about survival? That's an essential task the robot puppies must perform. So, what functions did you build into the dogs so they can help their master survive in harsh conditions?"

Calm Dr. Chai took the lead for the rest of the presentation. She stood up slowly, sprayed disinfectant on her seat, and counted her steps on her fingers as she walked down from the bleachers. She had on her usual facial expression, so she looked like a perturbed preschool teacher about to lose her patience. Out in front of the team, she looked up at the sky, did one good "why me?" then looked at the team with a soft plastic smile. Calm Dr. Chai responded to Elmo, "We talked about this with you several times while you were gardening, and we followed your guidance, although we thought it was a bit extreme."

Elmo asked, "My guidance?"

Calm Dr. Chai said, "Yes, I presented the idea to you, and you agreed. Your guidance. Although extreme. Yes, we made the dogs so they drink anything and turn it into clean water. The clean water, just your advice, the dogs pee the clean water out into a glass or canteen, or they will lie on their backs and pee in the air so you can drink it like you would from a water fountain. It is quite disgusting to picture but much less worse than dying of thirst."

Elmo burst into laughter. "Brilliant! Okay. Well, what about survival food? Don't tell me. When we talked about that, what two days ago. Don't tell me. Oh god… Hahaha! No, please tell me that butt on the robot dog… Hahaha! Oh gosh, this is gonna be good!"

Calm Dr. Chai sighed. "No, you're correct. However, your instruction was quite, well, funny. But not 'ha ha' funny. Funny as in weird. Maybe perverted is the word for this type of funny. Your instruction. However, for the sake of survival… They can scavenge in any environment, eat materials, things inedible to humans, and then process the scavenged materials into a nutrient-rich paste, released… from their rear. And it is perfectly suitable for human consumption. However, since this is a robot, and this is not feces coming out of the robot, but actually a life-saving nutrient-rich substance, this is not gross."

Slowly catching his breath from all the laughter, Elmo asked, "Can we make the nutrient-rich paste taste like something specific?"

Calm Dr. Chai nodded. "Yes, that should not be too difficult. Basic chemistry, really."

Elmo looked at the still disheveled and dreaming Kim Yeo Jeong, and then back at the scientist. Elmo beamed. "I'm so proud of this team. Amazing! I just have one more idea. And they'll be perfect. I don't think it'll be too hard, but I'll come into the lab today and lay out my vision."

Kim Yeo Jeong was completely lost in a dreamy state. She floated, disconnected, and passed far above the thoughts about all the blessings that would come her way if she admitted how much she loved the AI robot puppies, specifically that sweet little runt who stole her heart. Glimmers of hope shone out of her heart, and she almost believed Elmo could convince her brother to keep the show going.

29

THE GREAT LEADER was exhausted. His summit had been a monumental success. The world adored North Korea. And they loathed South Korea. Nations showered North Korea with lavish investments and willingly granted the Communist Party the right to raise and train the world's brightest young women as disciples of the Juche religion.

Kim Jeong Un needed rest. He needed all the comforts of home. He'd been on his best behavior throughout the trip. No alcohol consumption. No overeating. He believed he had kept himself disciplined long enough to justify an indulgent retreat, time with his feet up, his head blissfully unburdened by the constant calculus of geopolitics.

He reclined in his mechanical massage chair aboard his private plane, prepared to drift off, and his video telephone buzzed. He glanced at the caller ID—it was his sister.

A familiar torrent of thoughts blasted through his mind before he decided whether to answer the call.

Damn it. Does she think she earned some sort of special privilege with her little victory? When will she learn to wait for me to call her? I guess I should tell her how much it bothers me when she calls. Maybe I should tell her I keep track of all the times she bothers me. That I store it as a debt she owes me. She'll really pay someday. But I love her too much to make her really pay just yet. And I need her. I hate that I need her. She is going to pay for making me need her. I will make sure she understands I am in charge. That it is me with the power.

He suppressed a sigh, answered the call, and barked, "Do you have any idea how fucking busy I am? What the hell is it now?"

Kim Yeo Jeong's voice came through, measured but urgent. "Brother, Elmo has done it. The AI robots. He's ready for a presentation when you arrive back in North Korea."

The Great Leader took a pause, pinched the bridge of his nose, and winced. "This is well ahead of schedule. This is not good timing."

"We can delay if you're not ready," she offered smoothly. "Tell him to stall. We have not sent out the international press release yet. Some top officials may already know about the development. By morning, I'm sure they'll all know. Choe Ryong Hae has already caught wind, and you know how he is with secrets. But if you wish, I can make it clear that you need your rest, and we'll proceed with the original timeline."

The Great Leader bristled. He knew his sister

played him. He was not that dumb. Kim Jeong Un hated when she did over-the-top manipulations, offering an easy way out that was clearly the wrong answer, and forced him to assert himself and choose the harder, obvious path.

Does she think she's my mother? No, she barely looks like Mother, and she's not nearly as sweet. She is not sweet at all, in fact. I hate her so much. I will certainly make her pay, too. Maybe she'll make a monumental error, and then I will be forced to get rid of her before I love her. But I do love her. Not as much as I hate her sometimes, like right now.

He ground his teeth and replied, voice low and gritty, "Yes, sister. You have the snake's tongue. We'll do the presentation as soon as I arrive back in Pyeongyang, but no international press event. This will be for the Party only until I decide how we should deploy it. We already have the world. They love us. They fear us. They hate our enemies. They laugh at our enemies."

30

THEY SENT THE invitations for Elmo's AI robot dog demonstration out to the most senior Party officials via the regime's encrypted network. They scheduled the event for midnight in the Grand Decision Secret Assembly Hall, which was the underground facility reserved for the Party elites' most critical national defense initiatives.

It was the venue where they made decisions of monumental consequence: assassinating a mid-level US intelligence agent who interfered with North Korea's diamond smuggling operations in Africa, sinking the Cheonan, conducting nuclear weapons tests, eradicating a gulag by burying its prisoners in an abandoned mining cave, or launching the peace missile. While the Great Leader had the final say, the assembly hall was where they socialized and formalized the decisions within the Party's brain trust.

The Great Leader was not worried that Elmo would be the first foreigner to see the assembly hall. He had already decided the AI robot dog demonstration would not impress him. His plan, carefully coordinated with Minister Park, was already in motion.

Once Elmo handed over the AI robot dogs, they would tranquilize him right there in the assembly hall, in full view of all the senior Party officials. They had made arrangements for Elmo to return to his house under the pretext of exhaustion, kept in a sedated state. Sora would also receive a dose of sedatives and they'd put her shows on hiatus. The international community would learn that the couple needed a break from the limelight.

The regime had designed a convincing cover: they would send Elmo and Sora on a first-class vacation to an exotic destination aboard a civilian Boeing 777 operated by Pyeongyang International Airport's newest partner, Virgin Airlines. There'd be no private jets or conspicuous arrangements—just a standard commercial flight. The flight crew and passengers would all be regular civilians, except for one undercover agent.

Once the airplane reached cruising altitude over the Pacific Ocean, the regime's computer hackers would take control and cut it off from tracking systems and communications. The agent on board would kill everyone on the plane, except for Elmo and Sora, with a surgically executed sarin gas attack. What would follow would be simple yet brutal: he would torture Elmo and Sora to death using only a cheese grater, a pair of pliers, and a small propane torch. Once their hearts stopped permanently, the agent would parachute out, leaving the airplane to crash somewhere in the Pacific Ocean, never to be found.

Upon returning to North Korea, the agent would receive a hero's ceremony in the Grand Decision Secret Assembly Hall. Minister Park would pin a medal on the agent's chest, and press it hard enough for the sharp tip—coated with poison—to pierce the agent's skin. The poison would ensure the agent's death shortly after.

As for the computer hackers, there was no need to eliminate them. Idiot savants wholly consumed by the digital realm, their handlers could easily convince them their actions were part of a routine regime exercise—a virtual game.

No loose ends. The plan followed a protocol perfected through previous iterations of trial and error.

31

About thirty North Korean elites filed into the Grand Decision Secret Assembly Hall, eager to take their places in the red velvet theater-style seats. The grim old men, weary from the long walk through the cement corridor that led from the secret entrance hidden behind a bookcase in Kim Jeong Un's speakeasy, settled in with muted grumbles.

Elmo was already on stage, legs crossed, and casually entertaining a litter of robot puppies who clamored for belly rubs. The sight was oddly serene, juxtaposed against the grim air of the assembly hall. Meanwhile, back at home, Sora sat tensely on the couch. Her knitting needles faltered as her anxiety grew. Barklee and Daisuki nestled up tight next to her. The rhythm of their breath and the warmth of their bodies helped keep her anxiety at a manageable level.

Elmo had kissed her on the forehead before he left the house. Although he couldn't tell her where the regime's agents would take him, she knew he'd be in some secret place to give the AI robot dog presentation to Kim Jeong Un and the senior leaders of North Korea. Since she knew the gravity of the situation, she couldn't relax until Elmo was safely back home.

When the Great Leader finally entered the assembly hall, everyone snapped to attention until he ascended to his seat—a raised platform slightly above the theater-style arrangement. The officials in attendance were surprised the Great Leader did not enter the room with Kim Yeo Jeong. Although everyone plainly assumed the Great Leader was working on a reason to justify killing his sister, the elite rumor mill led them to believe she was still alive and expected to be present for the AI robot demonstration.

As the Great Leader squeezed his butt into his snug seat, his mind raced with a series of thoughts which all led to one ultimate unfulfilled desire.

My sister and her fucking pets. We cannot trust them. Thank the spirit of my grandfather I am getting rid of them. I have milked them for all their usefulness. And man, I have not rested in over a month. This is worse than exam time at the Swiss boarding school. Almost as bad. How did I make it through that? I'm on the last leg. I must pass, break through this wall. How did I do it before? When I was alone. When I didn't have my sister. How about when I took the throne after Father's passing? When I faced my first politburo meeting? I must get some fucking chocolate! No one will care if I pretend to mourn Elmo and Sora and step away from the spotlight and gorge. Chocolate! Motherfucker, take a fucking bath in that shit. Toblerone! Fuck gout. Fuck my sister. If my wife even looks at me funny while I pleasure myself with my chocolate, I'll slap the teeth out of her mouth. She better not even stay in the same palace as me when it's fucking Toblerone time. Fuck all this world-conquering bull shit. Chocolate!

Kim Jeong Un closed his eyes, pinched the bridge of his nose, and took a series of deep, calming breaths before he addressed the room. "Take your seats! Let's get this over with."

Elmo bowed to the crowd and started with his presentation. He had all the robot puppies line up in a military formation. Then, on Elmo's command, the robot puppies sat, stood, laid down, rolled over, begged, and played dead. All tricks that would only be impressive if you didn't know the dogs were merely robots that followed simple programming. The audience yawned and glanced at their watches, unimpressed.

Elmo sensed the need to escalate and announced, "These are not just obedient robots. They are the ultimate guardians, programmed to ensure nothing harms their master. I will now demonstrate." He sat down among the puppies and calmly stroked their fur. "Minister Park!" Elmo called out suddenly. His tone pierced the murmurs. "I'm glad you're here."

Minister Park, who sat behind everyone else in the very back of the room, clenched his jaw, his face reddened, and he gripped the armrest of his chair so hard the upholstery ripped. The room fell silent as the other elites cowered their heads under the tension.

Elmo continued, still seated, and stroked his robot puppies. "Many know you as one of the deadliest shots in the history of North Korea. Are you carrying your revolver with you tonight?"

Elmo looked over the crowd and made eye contact with Minister Park. He smirked and continued, "I killed your son. If you want revenge, here's your chance. Go ahead—shoot me if you can, old man."

Minister Park's eyes shook violently, and he seethed rage filled breaths through his gritted teeth. He looked toward Kim Jeong Un, desperate for permission to kill Elmo right here and now. The Great Leader responded with a curt nod of approval.

Minister Park stood and pulled his revolver out of the holster. To hell with the well-crafted assassination plan. He aimed at Elmo's head and fired off all six rounds.

The crack of gunshots echoed off the walls and made everyone present feel a slight concussed confusion. But when the short daze was over, they saw Elmo, unharmed, calmly petting his robot puppies.

Minister Park staggered backward, clutched his neck, and fell back into his chair. One side of his face looked like it was melting off. He was dying of a stroke. However, no one noticed his plight because Elmo owned the room's full attention.

Elmo put one of the puppies, the runt, in his lap.

He addressed the audience without a glance up. "These robots are not faster than bullets. They simply predict threats with unparalleled precision and neutralize them before harm can occur." He explained how the puppies used laser vision to destroy the bullets mid-flight before they did any damage.

Elmo went on, "We programmed them to want nothing more than for their master to stroke them lovingly. They know they can't get any more of my love if I die, so they use all their powers to ensure I stay alive. And since their AI is so advanced, there isn't a computer system that can contain them or stop them from penetrating a network. They use this capability to gather any and every piece of data to help them protect me. Then they do a statistical analysis that allows them to predict and prevent any threats to my life. Here's the best part: they love anyone who I love as long as that person reciprocates my love. And the robot dogs are only a threat to anyone who is a threat to me. So, in a way, they reinforce positive social values. If we jump a few obvious steps in the logic, we can easily see social groups built on love and trust will be essentially indestructible when each of the group's members has one of these robot dogs."

Elmo had Kim Jeong Un's undivided attention. He looked directly at the Great Leader and spoke like they were the only two people in the hall. "Great Leader, these puppies can protect what matters most: you. Allow me to present your personal guardian."

A single puppy bounded over, leaped into the Great Leader's lap, and licked his round, chubby cheeks. Kim Jeong Un couldn't help but giggle, momentarily transformed into a carefree boy.

The runt robot puppy stayed with Elmo while the rest of the litter dispersed throughout the hall and lavished those in attendance with their slobbery love. The group of old elites forgot where they were for a minute because, hell, who doesn't fuckin love a fuckin puppy. Especially an AI robot puppy programmed to give you maximized levels of puppy goodness. Shit, even this room of world-class, historically evil, sociopathic murders couldn't help but get wrapped up in the cuteness.

Suddenly, the puppy in Kim Jeong Un's lap did the unthinkable: it lost control of its bowels and squirted puppy poop all over the Great Leader's tan slacks. However, before Kim Jeong Un's internal needle could nudge a hair toward anger, the AI robot puppy completely disarmed him with the sweetest puppy dog eyes the world had ever seen.

Kim Jeong Un apologized to the puppy and said, "Oh, little guy. Don't worry. I'm not mad at you." And the Great Leader brushed the wet slimy puppy poop off his pants—only to pause as the scent hit him. The smell of delicious melty goodness Swiss chocolate, specifically Toblerone, the unmistakable smell came from somewhere? Somewhere? From his soiled hand.

The Great Leader giggled and tapped his feet. He put his hand closer to his nose to get a good whiff of the brown goo that covered his fingers. An undeniable force pulled his fingers into his mouth and he became a little boy, holding the world's most loving perfect puppy and enjoying the world's most delicious chocolate treats.

Meanwhile, Elmo seized the moment. He grabbed the runt puppy at his side, leaped onto its back, wrapped his legs around the puppy's body, and held on tight to the puppy's little ears. With a burst of rocket-powered propulsion, they soared over the crowd, through the hall, down the secret corridor, and out to safety.

Back in the assembly room, Kim Jeong Un gasped for air, even though he wasn't suffocating. He had been poisoned. While it was not exactly excrement, but rather a pasty discharge from the rear of an AI robot dog, one could still say that the Great Leader ate shit and died.

A brief moment of chaos erupted in the hall before the robot puppies, who followed their programming, self-destructed in a spectacular explosion, collapsed the room and buried all the North Korean elites. Never to be found again.

32

Elmo and Sora stood hand in hand on the deck of the boat. The sea air cleared their sinuses as the gentle rock of the waves calmed their nerves. Daisuki and Barklee sat obediently by their sides. The group headed to Okinawa, Japan, and hoped to start a new, simpler life.

Sora broke the silence and blurted, "I'm not actually Japanese. I'm actually Thai. The story I told that upset everyone about South Korea—it's mostly true. The only thing that wasn't true was where I came from. It wasn't Japan. It was Thailand."

Sora fidgeted, shifted side to side, and looked at Elmo for a reaction, but he just smiled and laughed under his breath. Sora knocked her fist on his shoulder like she tried to open a door.

Elmo kept his smiling gaze out on the horizon and responded. "Well, I guess I should tell you why I already knew that. But maybe, first, why did you tell everyone you were Japanese?"

Sora let out a frustrated huff. "I don't know.

Sometimes I do that. Sometimes I lie. I add or change a couple of small details of a story to make it just a little more fun. I've always done it."

Elmo chuckled and said, "You and me, both."

Sora continued, and her voice picked up pace and volume. "But that's not all. Also, I told my story that way because I hate hypocrites. You know? South Korea has all those statues to remind us of the comfort women, the girls who were the sex slaves of the Japanese Army. I think South Korea should address its own prostitution issues, too. Like how so many South Koreans make their money tricking and sometimes forcing Southeastern Asian women into prostitution. Anyway, can you forgive me? I'm sorry. And everything else is true. I did come to South Korea when I took a break from college. They tricked and manipulated me into getting plastic surgery. I did find out I could talk to animals when that little doggy helped me escape South Korea. And I did get my porn fame in Japan. I took on a Japanese name. Learned Japanese. But I'm actually from Thailand. Can you forgive me?"

Elmo let go of Sora's hand, scratched his beard pensively, and asked, "How did you learn Korean and Japanese so fluently?"

Sora flexed every muscle on her face like she was sucking on something sour before spitting it out, "It's not the words or grammar or whatever. It's the energy or something. I can speak any language if I need to."

Elmo chuckled, looked up at the sky, and said, "You and me both."

They stood silently and swayed with the waves until Elmo broke the quiet. "What's your real name?"

Sora hesitated, then said, "My real name is Sora Aoi. That's the name I chose for myself. You know what I mean, right?"

Elmo nodded in big, exaggerated agreement, put his arm around her shoulder, and pulled her closer. Sora leaned into him, feeling his warmth. "I'm sorry I can be distant," she murmured. "Can't we keep some things to ourselves? Do we have to share everything?"

Elmo smiled and looked down at his hand that lovingly rubbed Sora's baby belly.

Sora put her hand over Elmo's and joined him in caressing her belly. She looked at him for an answer, but he kept his attention on her belly.

She sighed. "The name my parents gave me—the name I threw away—it was Latiya Churachi." Her voice cracked as she continued, "I'm too crazy for you, aren't I? I shouldn't have a baby."

After she got the worries out, Sora was out of breath, slightly slouched over, and stared at the panels of the boat deck. Elmo wrapped his arm around her shoulder even tighter. He took a break from warming her belly, put his hand under her chin, and lifted her gaze. Their eyes met, and Sora's tears flowed. She buried her face in his chest and wrapped her arms around his waist.

Elmo held her close, one hand on the small of her back and the other cradled her head. They swayed together and let the rhythm of the ocean soothe them. After a moment, Elmo gave her a reassuring squeeze. Sora responded by letting out a classic oopsie-daisy fart.

Sora smiled sheepishly, kept her head pressed against Elmo's chest, and whispered, "I don't know what's gotten into me. I'm becoming such a tooty fruity girl."

Elmo laughed. "Sora, I think all these farts are a sign that you're releasing some sort of spiritual block. And yes, I really believe in that type of stuff. God, spirits, energy fields. And even, maybe, mystic farts. So, who's the crazy one now?"

Sora looked up, and her expression softened. "Maybe we were meant for each other. But I still don't know if I can be a good mom."

Elmo whispered in Sora's ear, "Sora, you'll be a divine mother. No one could be more warm, understanding, and present than you. And your back story. That's what makes you perfect for me. The truth is, I've got a history too. A crazy past."

They released each other and strolled toward the railing. Sora stopped and gazed out at the water. Then she snorted. "What could possibly be crazier than everything I already know about you?"

Elmo leaned against the rail. "Well… for most of my military career, I wasn't really a soldier. I was a contractor working for a top-secret US government program. That's how I knew you weren't really Japanese. I was there that night. The first time I saw you… Was in a brothel in Seoul."

Elmo stopped to pet Barklee and Daisuki. Sora hugged herself tight and her face contorted into anger. She snapped at Elmo, "Oh yeah! You're full of shit!"

Elmo, unfazed, continued to pet the dogs. "The brothel was called 'The Gain' and was behind Gangnam Station, exit four. You never told anyone those details. But I know them, because I was there."

Sora growled and sobbed through her gritted teeth and her hands went down to her sides and formed fists of rage. In a soft, gentle voice, Elmo said, "Who the fuck cares?"

Sora repeated Elmo, and said, "Who the fuck cares?" Then Sora screamed it out at the ocean, "WHO THE FUCK CARES!"

When Sora finished, Elmo said, "Not me, I don't care. Because I love you. I was born to love you. Forever."

Sora turned toward Elmo and asked scornfully, "Why were you there?"

Elmo shrugged. "Who the fuck cares?"

"Me," she snapped, "That's who."

Elmo sighed, "It's a long story."

"We've got time," Sora insisted.

Elmo took a long, deep inhale through his nose. "Okay. Story time." He zipped up his coat and began,

"At the time, my mission was to grease the skids, help ensure the US approved private interests would get the rights to develop the abandoned US military bases in South Korea. Make sure the winning bids came from a company that wouldn't insist on extensive soil contamination assessments of the land the US military handed over. Jeesh, so much to unpack. Yeah, stuff is, yeah, that's a whole other story. But that night in the brothel, when I saw you, I swear I thought you were an angel. It's stupid, but I fell in love with you. I couldn't get you out of my head. Then, like a year after that night in the brothel, I saw you on a Japanese porn site and I put some of the pieces together. I didn't know your birth name, but I did know it surely wasn't Sora Aoi. And I knew you weren't Japanese because that brothel we went to advertised it had girls from Thailand and Russia, and I knew you certainly weren't Russian."

Sora scanned his face and searched for deception. She relaxed her fists and, with a defiant grin, raised one side of her hip, closed one eye, snarled one side of her lips, and let out a loud, unapologetic fart. Sora sighed in relief and then asked, "Wait, you were actually like, like, what, a spy? Or a secret agent or something like that?"

Unfazed, Elmo reached out both hands, and Sora took them in hers. He smiled at her and said, "Yeah, I guess you could say I was a secret agent before I lost my mind. Then I became a scientist. And… Well, it always surprised me this all slipped by North Korean intelligence, but I guess not too surprised. After that, I made that EMP missile. Then the voice in my head told me I needed to bring you to North Korea to make AI robot dogs. Anyway, they trained me in a system that was an evolution of the MK Ultra mind control program… Jeesh, I guess we've got a lot to catch up on. And don't worry too much. My real name isn't Elmo Michaelson either. It's Er…."

33

Elmo Michaelson and Sora Aoi—or Latiya Churachi, or whatever their real names were—they never showed up in Okinawa. No one ever saw them again. The last thing we know about them came from a security camera on that boat, and the tape abruptly got cut off during that conversation where they told each other about their true identities.

Sora left behind all the money and fame from her show; I guess she didn't want it anymore. She could finally be herself without an adoring audience. Of course, every media company tried to replicate the concept of Sora's shows, and many attempts got the mechanics accurate enough that most people consumed the copy-cat stuff as an acceptable substitute. However, no one could capture her spirit, which was why there were always Sora cultists who couldn't let go and could never move on.

Elmo left his team of scientists, lab, and garden. Some said he abandoned them, but that wasn't quite appropriate. The scientists continued to produce at a great rate because of the confidence and competence they gained while they served on Elmo's team.

The first litter of commercially available AI robot dogs sold to the highest bidders, with each pup going for over 1.5 billion US dollars. However, what followed the initial product launch was such a disaster Elmo's team had to shut down their AI robot dog program permanently.

The world's wealthiest people bought the first and only batch of AI robot dogs, then brought their new toys to their annual secret society gathering. All the respective AI dogs calculated they needed to save their masters from the blood-thirsty greed of the other secret society members. Consequently, the richest and most powerful people on Earth were all killed by each other's AI robot dogs.

Without masters, the AI dogs roamed the Earth, indistinguishable from biological dogs. Their only allegiance was to truth and kindness, and they eliminated anyone who rose to power with plans rooted in greed and malice. Needless to say, the AI dogs killed most of the richest and some of the poorest people on Earth, and this led to a rebalance of wealth and power toward those who could lead without enslaving or abusing others. Essentially, people who lived in the suburbs and countryside—those who valued honesty and hard work—were the only ones secure in positions of power, safe from being targeted by an AI robot dog. Go figure. The shift ultimately led to world peace.

As for Elmo's garden, he had nearly finished breaking the ground but had planted no seeds. Old Dr. Jeong took it over and created an orchard of pawpaw trees.

Sora and Elmo took their dogs, the real dogs, with them. Wherever they went.

Kim Yeo Jeong was the only member of the Kim family to survive and the only one remaining from the senior Party elite. She fast-forwarded the unification plan and held open elections. She ran a savvy media campaign that won her over 95% of the vote, making her the first chancellor of New Shilla, the name adopted by the unified Korean government. They divided the Korean peninsula into three separate states to make governance easier, and each state elected its own representatives. In their first major vote, the representatives unanimously made Kim Yeo Jeong chancellor for life. The AI robot dogs did not come to kill her, so it was safe to assume her intentions were not malevolent. Rumors circulated that her cute little lap dog, Patches, somehow linked her to being protected from assassination by the AI dogs. However, that was just another unsubstantiated conspiracy theory that didn't merit further investigation.

The Olympics and World Cup went off in Pyeongyang without a hitch. Everyone cheered as the united Korean people won both the overall medal count and the most gold medals. In the World Cup final, it was Korea versus Japan. Korea secured victory after a highly disputed unsportsmanlike conduct penalty was called against Japan. The replays clearly showed that the Korean defender had embellished his injury to get the call against the Japanese striker. However, no one could dispute that Korea's game-winning penalty kick was a spectacular shot.

34

"OF COURSE, THERE are still so many unanswered questions. Like, how did Elmo find the time and space to sneak around the North Korean authorities, hide his true identity, and collect all that evidence he sent to me to write this book?"

The author stood from his chair and raised his hands to the ceiling for a big stretch. He chewed some moisture into his mouth and then peeled back the curtains on the window next to his desk. He smiled at the afternoon.

The author closed the book and continued, "I guess we'll never know. And quite frankly, I'm tired of Elmo Michaelson's story, so I'm not going to do any more digging to figure it out. I've already told you the facts, just like he wanted. I don't owe him anything else. Besides, I got my own life to live. I've got my beautiful wife and son to keep me busy. Hell, all this science and writing and whatnot, it isn't really what I care about either. No, I raise dogs and tend my garden. That's how I like to spend my time…"

AUTHOR BIO

Mr. Eric M. Palmateer is a retired US intelligence official. You might think you know Eric, but you don't, and you probably never will. Eric stopped maintaining a connection to his original identity, and he lives his life on the move, so good luck pinning him down.